The Good Cyclist

DIRK BUDWILL

A realistic and authentic portrait of the struggles that a typical soldier of World War 1 may have experienced. Provides interesting insight into the mental anguish of the men and women who lived through the Great War through the eyes of the main character, Ludwig Schmidt.

Kylie Barnstable
Chaplain/Educator

The Good Cyclist is a very interesting and enjoyable book. It is a real page turner. I am now using portions of the book for my history classes. I had my students' read the Sept 28th 1914 entry. They then prepared a 2 minute presentation on one of four topics (based on the suggestions from *The Good Cyclist* teacher packet.) The students really enjoyed it and came up with good points in their speeches. From that I did a lesson on the Just War Theory. "*The Good Cyclist*," is an excellent resource for social studies or history teachers and students studying about war. It helps them understand the concept of "jus in bello" – which concerns whether a war is conducted justly. *The Good Cyclist* is a book I will read again and share.

Marg Fleishauer
Professional Educator

How can a person maintain a sense of all that is good and right while killing others, or even dealing with conflicts between peers? Ludwig Schmidt, the protagonist of "*The Good Cyclist*," fights more the battle within himself than the conflict, (World War I), he is engaged in for his country. He soon realizes that while the war sucks up all his physical energy, it also challenges everything a loving family has taught him. As you read this book about the struggles that face Ludwig Schmidt, be prepared to do battle within yourself as you imagine yourself in the same position, making the same choices. Dirk Budwill has done an amazing work in dealing with our internal struggles, our faith, and our relationship with the redeemer of this place called a turbulent and violent earth.

Chris Solomon
Writer, newspaper columnist and head of
Potters Hands kitchen ministry.

The Good Cyclist is an intimate and intense account of a Christian man's battle with the evil that is conspired against him. With plenty of action, historical facts, romance, and Christian ethical conflict the book will keep a reader engaged throughout. I highly recommend *The Good Cyclist*.

Celia Rigodon
Educator

The Good Cyclist is an elegantly written, heartbreaking story. I read the book in one sitting. Dirk gives so many insights about World War 1, which are ignored by the media or the government.

The emphasis of the book is very much on human emotions, and Dirk does an excellent job in allowing the letters written by Ludwig Schmidt to tell their stories.

The main strength of the book is how Ludwig expresses his faith in God. The shame and pain that Ludwig experiences can only be washed away by God's love.

Helen Ganbaatar
Professional Educator
Good evening!

I am the Acquisition Manager at 5Fold Media and I did your original review when you had sent in your manuscript for *The Good Cyclist*. I fell in love with it, but never got to do anything but review it. I just purchased the ebook and devoured the final product! What an amazing story! It was brilliant!

God bless!

Ps. Keep writing!

Kathy Dolman
Acquisition Manager, 5Fold Media

Contents

Foreword

War is a destroyer of man. It is quite honestly a desired and perpetuated conflict between leaders who use the most valuable resource that they have—their citizens—in order to take what does not belong to them.

Glory and honor awaits those who battle well. Accolades are profuse for those who excel at the craft of killing the opposition and/or protecting their own; there is no shortage of recognition for those who excel at this insidious game. No amount of training or conditioning prepares a person for the utter devastation caused by war—the death, the mutilation, the senseless destruction of homes and lands. Additionally, nothing can prepare a person's heart and mind for the battle within. How can a person maintain a sense of all that is good and right while killing others or even dealing with conflicts between peers.

Ludwig Schmidt fights the battle within himself more than the conflict he is engaged in for his country. He soon realizes that while the war sucks up all his physical energy, it also challenges everything a loving family has taught him. Coupled with physical disfigurement, the rejection he feels tests everything he knows about faith in a loving and caring God, and the taunting from his peers almost takes him away from that faith.

Having studied God's Word with the author, I realize that this writing is not only about the internal conflict that Ludwig Schmidt deals with; it is also about us and the challenges we face daily in our walk with a loving and merciful Saviour—challenges that threaten to take away our faith and also attempt to make us voluntarily set aside our faith.

As you read this book about the struggles that face Ludwig Schmidt, be prepared to do battle within yourself as you imagine yourself in the same position, making the same choices. Dirk Budwill has done an amazing work in dealing with our internal struggles, our faith, and our relationship with the Redeemer of this turbulent and violent earth in which we live.

— Chris Salomons

Chris Salomons is a founding member of Potter's Hands Ministries in Red Deer, Alberta, Canada and serves as kitchen coordinator for the ministry. Potter's Hands Ministries is committed to demonstrating the love of Jesus Christ in tangible ways, as outlined by our Lord: *"for I was hungry and you gave Me food; I was thirsty and you gave Me drink; I was a stranger and you took Me in"* (Matthew 25:35). Chris Salomons also writes a regular column in the *Red Deer Advocate* called "Street Tales.

Prologue

The assassination on 28 June, 1914 of Archduke Franz Ferdinand of Austria, heir to the Austro-Hungarian throne, by a Serbian nationalist was the spark that ignited World War I. Austro-Hungary's resulting demands against the king of Serbia activated a sequence of alliances. These alliances compelled countries to fight and defend an ally if they were threatened by an opposing power. Germany entered the conflict as a key defender of the Austro-Hungarian Empire. Ludwig Schmidt, a young German man, was conscripted by the German army to battle the Russians on the Eastern Front.

World War I Facts

1. The spark that ignited World War I was the assassination of Archduke Franz Ferdinand of Austria, heir to the Austro-Hungarian throne, by a Serbian nationalist on 28 June, 1914. Austro-Hungary's resulting demands against the king of Serbia activated a sequence of alliances. These alliances compelled countries to fight and defend an ally as if they were threatened by an opposing power.

2. World War I (WWI) also known as the First World War, the Great War, and the War to End All Wars, was a global military conflict that involved most of the world's great powers. Countries such as the United States, Canada, Great Britain, France, and Russia fought against Germany and Austro-Hungary.

3. World War I lasted from 1914-1918 and took place mainly in the European countries of France, Belgium, Germany, and

Russia. Seventy million military personnel were activated for the war. Fifteen million people died.

4. World War I was called a total war because the nations involved devoted their entire scientific and industrial capabilities into the war effort.

5. Airplanes, tanks, and poisonous gas were first used in WWI.

6. Trench warfare was introduced in WWI. Opposing armies built open tunnels in the ground to shield themselves from opposing gunfire and to provide a rallying point for an attack against the opposing army.

7. There were two fronts where the majority of the battles took place during WWI. The Western Front, located primarily in Belgium and France, was for the most part trench warfare. This was due to its short length and high concentration of opposing military forces. As a result warfare was static with armies "entrenched" for months in one location.

8. The Eastern Front was located mainly in Russia, and stretched for approximately 900 kilometers from the Baltic to the Black Sea. Since this front was so long, it did not have the same high concentration of men and military equipment as the Western Front and subsequently did not have as many trenches. As a result it was impossible to maintain a position for too long on the Eastern Front, so both opposing armies, German and Russian, took turns making great advances into each other's territories. The Eastern Front was thus considered more fluid as compared to the static Western Front.

9. The United States did not enter World War I until 1917 due to its isolationist policies.

10. At war's end, four imperial powers—the German, Russian, Austro-Hungarian, and Ottoman empires—were either defeated militarily or politically. Austro-Hungary and the Ottoman Empire ceased to exist.

11. The League of Nations was organized to prevent another conflict like WWI.

12. Despite the efforts of the League of Nations to prevent another world war, other forces overrode its effectiveness. European nationalism, the repercussions of Germany's defeat, and the requirements of the Treaty of Versailles on Germany would lead to World War II in 1939.

Do not be overcome by evil, but overcome evil with good.

— Romans 12:21

22 August 1914

Ostrode, East Prussia (near the Russian Front)

Dear Elise,

I left with the 31st Company on a train from the Lüebeck station in fairly good spirits. However, riding for hours in a cramped, muggy, hot compartment left everyone smelling terrible, dehydrated, exhausted, and in despicable foul moods. When we finally arrived in Ostrode, East Prussia, I thought things would get better. I was sadly mistaken. It was greenhouse hot and humid. A few men swooned flat on their backs once they stepped off the train. The leader of our military operation, Lieutenant Colonel (Oberstleutnant) Speck, showing no mercy, bellowed out orders that our muddled minds had trouble grasping.

Suddenly the sound of cannons thundered nearby, drowning out the plump lieutenant colonel's demands. Like young does startled by a hunter, many of us scattered for cover under the train. This absolutely infuriated Speck, causing him to brandish a short horse whip. Lashing it at anyone and everyone within his vicinity, our rotund superior eventually managed to restore some semblance of order. Roll call was taken. When Speck was assured of my presence, he immediately ordered me to step forward.

A black bicycle was wheeled toward me by a man named Sergeant (Unteroffizier) Schwarz. His face sneered at me with disdain. Schwarz respected my ability as a cyclist, but did not believe I was a good soldier. As a result of this belief we had developed a mutual distaste for one another. My interactions with the sergeant often bristled with unspoken tension. Schwarz brought the bicycle near to me, then let it drop at my feet. Speck glared at the sergeant for a moment but didn't say anything. Schwarz melted back into the line of soldiers who were panting in the oppressive heat like dogs.

Speck came up and spat out his orders directly into the scarf that, along with dark glasses, hid my deformed face. He did not appear to be at all taken aback by my odd appearance. Not an extra stare or condescending word. Nothing. I appreciated this since it was in front of the entire company. Speck was treating me like anyone else. Poorly, but at least it wasn't due to my disfigurement. Speck demanded that I bike ahead to the front, where the 47th was engaged in battle, and advise any surviving military leaders (Kommandants) that reinforcements had arrived. Then I was to hurry back and report on the situation at hand. With my rifle strapped to the bicycle, I hurriedly pedaled off, heading east toward the sound of thunder and the glow of fire.

Ostrode was empty of civilians. It was obvious that they had fled for their lives. I passed their homes and businesses in the throes of destruction; some were completely demolished, while others still had a few walls standing. I came out of the village and entered a forest. An abrupt rain shower relieved the discomfort of the heat and what I had just seen in Ostrode. Slowly I moved forward with my head tilted up. As water gushed down my throat and splashed coolly over my weary head, I experienced a mild revival. The outburst of precipitation couldn't have lasted more than ten minutes. When it stopped the pines emitted a fragrance that made me stop and take long, life-giving breaths.

Boom! Boom! A sudden artillery blast abruptly ended the moment. My feet spun the pedals forward. A queasy, flu-like sensation came over me. For the next several months this feeling would haunt me constantly. It was fear. Fear of the unknown, fear of reprimand from leaders, fear of ridicule from comrades, fear of a gruesome injury or death.

The cannons suddenly stopped. The silence that came over the forest was eerie. Where were the birds? There was no wind. The only sounds I could hear were the crunching of the bicycle's tires against gravel and my own labored breathing. The anxiety that had been heating my mind like water slowly coming to a boil increased as the forest slowly gave way to a meadow. Why was there no sound?

Pop! Crash!

I flew headfirst off the bicycle and landed in a heap. For several minutes I laid there, face first on the gravel, too stunned to move. Gingerly I pushed myself up to a sitting position. The bicycle lay nearby, its front tire mutilated into several crazy angles. I remained sitting for several seconds, letting my mind clear, and then slowly, unsteadily, I lifted my aching bones up. Upon inspection of the tire it became clear what had happened. A piece of razor-sharp shrapnel, embedded in the trail and thus barely discernible, had pierced the front tire causing the air inside the tube to explode like a child's balloon.

Silence. Was I deaf? I spoke to myself. No, I wasn't deaf. I freed my rifle from the riggings on the demolished bicycle and got it ready to fire. With tender, careful steps I moved from the forest into a meadow.

Horror!

I dropped to one knee as my head spun. Collecting myself I stood up and stared in disbelief at the scene before me. At least five hundred soldiers, half German, half Russian, lay strewn helter-skelter over the wildflowers and lush green tall grass. They were all dead. Some looked quite peaceful, as if they were having a late afternoon nap, while others had been obliterated beyond recognition. Body parts, smoking artillery, guns, and pieces of clothing were scattered between the corpses. And silence. The silence was a thick, smothering blanket. How many of these sons, fathers, uncles, and brothers would be mourned over? How many lives were now changed forever because of this slaughter? Terrible.

Something unusual caught my eye. A bicycle? Yes, a fine black military bicycle. Yet there was something different about it. Upon further inspection, and based on my knowledge of military bicycles, I came upon the startling conclusion that my fortuitous discovery was English. How did an English military bicycle get to the Eastern Front? The Russians were allies with the English, so no doubt that was the reason. After strapping my rifle onto the riggings of the newly discovered treasure, I lifted it up, got on, and started pedaling. It was beautiful. Much better than the one I was given at the train station. I decided that I would not tell anyone that my new bicycle was English for fear of confiscation. There was no doubt in my mind that everyone in my company would not notice the difference anyway.

Suddenly it dawned on me that I wasn't sure whether this was the front or not. Where was I? Where were the Russians? More importantly, where were the Germans? The firing of nearby cannons made the decision straightforward. I pedaled quickly away from the sound and headed back where I had come from. The day's light began to fade, but I was extra careful, watching the ground intently for shrapnel.

Eventually, I found Speck at a slightly damaged home on the outskirts of Ostrode. He started screaming at me as soon as he saw me. "Where have you been, we have been waiting for hours, you are a sorry excuse for a soldier," and so on.

When he finally took a breath I calmly said, "They're dead."

This comment cluttered Speck's mind for a moment and he paused his tirade to croak out a "What?"

"They're dead. At least I think the company you sent me to is dead. Where is the front?"

I should not have asked that.

Speck regained his fury and blasted me for being such a useless soldier. "Any nincompoop should know where the front is and much more."

Thankfully Speck did not notice my new bicycle was English. I am sure he would have found that yet another reason to be angry.

Needless to say, it was now dark, I was hungry, the cannons were quiet, and fatigue suddenly came over me, dimming my brain. I was mercifully dismissed by Speck and ordered to enter the house's kitchen for a meal. I found some leftover goose that my company had devoured hours earlier.

I dug up a potato in the small garden behind the house and ate ravenously. It was delicious. I explored the house for a place to sleep but every nook and cranny was filled with snoring, stinking men. I stumbled outside and let the moon guide me to a small shed in the corner of the garden. I cleared out some tools, found some hay, made a small nest, and before giving in to sleep, I wrote to you, Elise. I also prayed and reminisced about when we met.

On January 8, 1914, at 10:17 in the morning I saw you for the first time. You were selling chocolates to some children at the Maier Chocolate Shop. At first I could not grasp your beauty. Golden hair, perfect delicate nose, full red lips that highlight lovely white teeth. And your skin! Smooth, white porcelain. And your height and figure? Angelic! On that day, when I came into the shop to deliver parcels and letters for Herr Maier, you saw me and your eyes, unlike hundreds of others, did not register horror or fear at my strange appearance. Only warmth. Then you smiled. I tried to whisper hello, but it wouldn't come out. Herr Maier arrived and I awkwardly dropped the bills and packages on the floor as I tried to hand them over. He screamed his disappointment at me and my tip was significantly smaller that day. Yet your smile and warm eyes were from heaven.

Every Thursday for almost five months I cycled to the Maier Chocolate Shop with bills and parcels for Herr Maier, and there you were behind the counter selling chocolates to young and old, your face aglow like morning sunshine. And every time I came into the shop, you said hello to me with your eyes. I always tried to respond, but the words never came. Thank you for your kindness. I believe you saw a glimpse of a man, a man who wants to love and be loved. Yet, the fire destroyed my human shell and I have come to believe my appearance is too horrible for anyone to love me.

Instead I can only dream.

Ludwig

23 August 1914

Dear Elise,

This morning I led Speck and the others of the 31st to the battlefield I stumbled on yesterday. The heat of the day made the stench from the rotting, bloated corpses almost unbearable. Birds had pecked away at the bodies, making them even more grotesque. We set about scavenging the dead for ammunition, food, clothing, guns, anything and everything that might help our cause.

The sudden crack of a gun and the agonizing cry of the one whose leg had absorbed a Russian bullet caused us all to sprawl nose first to the ground. Bullets hailed over us. Speck screamed to fire back. Five soldiers of the 31st stood up and tried, but they were cut down simultaneously; their expired bodies crumpled to the ground in bizarre angles. Speck frantically yelled for us to retreat and we slithered back on our bellies. Low-flying bullets, however, thudded into several bodies and screams of agony pierced our eardrums. Men were dying all around me.

I glanced back and froze in terror.

Like shadows they drifted out of the forest from the east. Russian soldiers, seemingly, hundreds of them. They attacked us while letting out a terrifying cry, like wolves who are about to tear up a cornered deer. I lay among the corpses too frightened to move. The screaming Russians passed over me, but then suddenly they reversed their run. Five German machine guns hidden in the western forest, the one we had come out of initially, opened fire dropping the Russians like wooden string puppets that had just been let go by their human handlers. The onslaught lasted a few seconds, but I remained face down on the ground for much longer.

Finally, I dared to raise my head. Smoke and corpses came into view. It was strangely silent until suddenly Sergeant Schwarz emerged out of the smoke and upon seeing me, with five other survivors, bellowed, "Schmidt!"

I picked myself up, saluted, and croaked, "yes, sir!"

Schwarz glared at my scarf-covered face with unconcealed disgust as he demanded, "Did you shoot back Schmidt! Did you fight?"

"No, sir," I stammered. "I couldn't get at my rifle."

Schwarz spit out, "A warrior would have no excuses. They would have sacrificed their lives for their Kaiser and for their comrades!" The sergeant paused and let his last words hang heavy in the air. The other men stood stiffly and quietly nearby. Then with some scorn, "At least you can ride a bicycle. Here take this money and buy these men, these true soldiers some beer! Off you go now." Humiliated, I pedaled off on my bicycle. Many unpleasant and ungodly thoughts toward Schwarz seethed through my mind.

After a long and arduous ride to the west, well past Ostrode, I finally found a small store in a tiny village that had suffered only slight damage from the war. The scarf that concealed me from the world had gotten dirty during the battle and was impossible to wear. Only the dark glasses covered my eyes, but this was not enough to prevent a look of disdain from the storekeeper as he looked at my mutilated face. As politely as possible I ordered beer from him. Yet, as so often happens with people who do not know me, he misinterpreted my weak voice as disrespect and yelled at me to speak up. For some odd reason I tried. Desperately. To no avail. The smoke from the fire had permanently ruined my vocal cords. More yelling from the storekeeper ensued.

I placed the money on the counter. It was more than enough and I refused change from the livid storekeeper. That gesture calmed him down somewhat. I quickly put the beer in a large empty rucksack and threw it, with much effort, for it was very heavy, on my back. My spine screamed for relief, but I didn't care. My job was to bring refreshments for the soldiers of my company.

The whole process of getting the beer had taken me several hours and it was well into the evening when I arrived back in Ostrode and returned to the slightly damaged house that the company had taken refuge in. The owners of this home had long fled for safety to the west.

Schwarz welcomed me back with disappointment: "What took you so long, Schmidt?" I stared back with anger billowing in my soul and mumbled, "It was difficult to find the beer sir." Schwarz lifted the rucksack roughly from my back and inspected the contents. He pulled out a beer, popped the cap off with his belt buckle, took a swig and bellowed. "The beer is as warm as mother's milk! Not acceptable!" He walked up to me and he lifted his right hand to strike my face.

Suddenly, a shrill command of "Halt!" stopped Schwarz like a man running full flight into a wall. It was the captain of the 31st, (Hauptmann) Lichtwasser, and his face was creased with lines of concern. He came up to Schwarz. "Did Private Schmidt follow your orders, sergeant?"

Schwarz paused for a moment and quietly, averting eye contact, said, "No, sir."

"Look at me when you answer, sergeant!"

Schwarz raised his head and repeated, "No, sir!"

"What did he do wrong?" asked the captain.

"He did not bring provisions back to us in a timely fashion, sir!"

Lichtwasser looked at the rucksack with the beer that I had, with great physical effort, brought to them. He snatched the beer out of Schwarz's hand and studied it. "You are reprimanding Private Schmidt for not bringing beer on time?"

Schwarz remained quiet. "Answer me sergeant!"

"Yes, sir. It is warm, sir."

Lichtwasser took a long, hearty swig from Schwarz's beer and then spat it out violently on the floor. "On that point you are absolutely correct, sergeant. It is much too warm."

Schwarz's crow eyes narrowed into steely slits. He started vibrating slightly, so great was his anger at Lichtwasser. The captain walked up to the sergeant, stared into the slits, and exploded. "You were about to strike Private Schmidt for bringing you warm beer! Fool! We need him to bring important messages and orders along this front! Our very lives depend on it! Sergeant Schwarz, the next time you reprimand Schmidt, or anyone else in this company for not getting beer to you in a timely fashion, I'll have you personally digging my trench for the rest of the war. Idiot!" Lichtwasser paused, caught his breath, and very quietly said, "Now, thank the private sergeant."

"What?"

"Are you deaf? Thank him!

Schwarz gulped out, "Yes, sir." He turned to me and in a monotone said, "Thank you."

Lichtwasser looked at me and said firmly, so everyone could hear, "Please know I respect you and your abilities, Private Schmidt."

"Thank you, sir," I rasped.

Lichtwasser turned to Schwarz and in a tone that barely masked his disgust for the sergeant said, "Private Ludwig Schmidt is an important part of this company. So far, to the best of my knowledge, he has done his job as a cyclist with exemplary effort. Unless he fails to do that, Sergeant Schwarz, you and everyone here is to treat Private Schmidt with the respect of a soldier and a human being. Understand?"

Schwarz responded meekly, "Yes, sir."

Lichtwasser glared at the other soldiers. "That goes for everyone!" "Yes sir!" They bellowed in unison.

Lichtwasser stared at Schwarz for the longest time with blazing eyes before he demanded, "Get a mop and wipe my spit off the floor! Now!"

Schwarz obeyed. Then the captain strode off to attend to other duties.

An awkward silence ensued. It eventually was broken when, one by one, the soldiers Schwarz had promised beer to, came up to me. They nodded or said their thanks, and took a beer or two from my rucksack. I was eventually all alone with Schwarz. I did not look back at him as I left him mopping the floor. However, I knew deep down that Schwarz's humiliation would not bode well for me in the future. I went to the shed and crawled into my nest early. The rest of the company sat outside, around a raging fire, laughing, telling stories, enjoying each other's company. I thanked God for Captain Lichtwasser. As the murmuring voices of the 31st Company comfortably lulled me to sleep, I wrote to you, my angel, Elise.

Once, before the fire, I was a handsome young boy. That was what everyone said. I was deeply loved by my mother and father. Before the fire I had a younger sister who I fought with and loved as most normal siblings do. Before the fire my mother read to me every night. The stories were always of men who would become heroes because they stayed true to what is good. As I drifted off to sleep I could hear my mother's soothing voice.

I was loved.

Every morning mother would begin the day by reading Bible passages to me and my sister. Later, after the fire, I would find life again in the Bible. My father was a schoolmaster. He was stern, but fair. He loved books; he loved to write; he loved to ride his bicycle. By the time I was five my father had taught me how to read, write, and ride a bicycle. Many times during the sweet months of spring, summer, and fall my father, in the lead on a magnificent black bicycle, and myself, on a much smaller version following just behind, would head for a forest. The citizens of Lüebeck were always impressed with our little parade and many gave us bemused respect—a bow, a doffing of a hat, a slight wave, wide smiles, and twinkling eyes as we rolled past them.

In the forest father would teach me about plants and animals; we'd snooze in the sunshine; and he'd tell me stories. Many, many, wonderful stories.

I was loved.

Ludwig

29 August 1914

Dear Elise,

Word of how Captain Lichtwasser made Sergeant Schwarz apologize to me flew through the 31st like a hungry hummingbird flitting from flower to flower. The men have a healthy respect for Lichtwasser and his words and actions carry great clout. As a result, they have been noticeably quiet around me. The stupid stares and taunts that I endured at basic training from the men of the 31st have dissipated. Being ignored is certainly an improvement from being tormented. I am so grateful to Captain Lichtwasser.

My duties have been expanded. No longer am I simply a messenger and procurer of goods, but I am also a mailman. Every day, when possible, I travel deep into Germany to deliver and then retrieve large mail bags for not only the 31st but other companies that are stationed near our position. The reaction of the men on my return is interesting. Concern if I bring an order to march or attack, joy if all I bring is the post. Most men receive several letters and even packages. Quiet tears are often shed as they read or hold their treasures from home. It is obvious that the men crave the affections of their families and desperately long to be reunited with them. Only Schwarz and I seem to be exempt from this bittersweet situation. I always imagine what you, Elise, might write to me and this gives me some solace. Schwarz's face, on the other hand, registers pain when he receives his one, and it is invariably only one, letter. His ritual with it is always the same— twirl the letter once with his right hand and then, without opening, tear iit in half before throwing the remains in the nearest garbage or fire. It is obvious that Schwarz is upset. Why? Maybe someday I will know.

I turned 22 today. No one knew. No one acknowledged my birth, let alone my existence. Ten years ago, during a late summer night, when my family and I were asleep in our beds, the *fire* swept through the home where I was loved. The heat of the *fire* woke me up and I yelled and yelled for my family to wake up. It was too late. The *fire* destroyed my parents and sister; their screams as they tried to escape the flames haunt me still. The *fire* consumed my body and configured my face into such an ugly shape that to this day I can't show emotion with my mouth. I inhaled too much smoke in the fire and it reduced my voice to a scratchy rasp. The *fire* left me in an inhuman shell, but underneath this abomination of skin, I am human. The *fire* transported me from a life of love, security, and joy to one of torment, loneliness, and poverty. I spent a year as an invalid in a sanitarium recovering from the burns that covered ninety percent of my body. The stay there depleted what little money my father had left me. Relatives came and went to visit; not one took me in after I was allowed to leave. I was ugly, destitute, and alone. I was twelve years old.

An orphanage became my new home. Despite my excellent records as a student, schools, including my father's, refused to take me in. Educators considered me physically incapable of spending a day in a school environment. Just as well. The horror of my mutilated flesh would have been too much of a distraction for the teachers and students.

Thankfully, there were many books at the orphanage and I read voraciously, only leaving my room during times when I knew there would not be many people outside. The disgust people expressed due to my appearance was conveyed by odd stares, taunts, and mocking laughter. This tore at my being and left me emotionally tattered. I retreated into a fantasy world, reading constantly about love, adventure, heroes, virtue, honesty, good and evil. I lived in those stories. I read the Bible as well. It brought me back to a place, a memory where I was loved. Finally, I developed my writing skills and wrote stories in which I was a hero. I was admired.

One marvelous spring day, close to my eighteenth birthday, I ventured outside the orphanage and found a discarded bicycle in the alley nearby. The wheels were damaged, but after some diligent effort I managed to straighten them into a reasonable shape. I hadn't ridden a bicycle since the fire, but the skills came back easily. I put on a hat, scarf, and dark glasses to hide my grotesque face and rode constantly. I would often bike into a forest and hide underneath a giant oak tree. Once I was settled, I dreamt, read, and wrote. God, books, writing, and the bicycle became my freedom and made me strong—mind, body, and soul.

One day the head of the orphanage asked me to deliver a message to an acquaintance. Covering my head as usual with a hat, glasses, and a scarf, I rode my bicycle and delivered the message so fast that I received a tip. Shortly thereafter, this same person hired me to deliver an important letter to a business associate. One thing led to another and soon I was delivering parcels, letters, bills, and messages between several different people and businesses, all for a small tip each time I made a delivery. The faster I rode my bicycle, the more tips I got. The tips multiplied rapidly, allowing me to buy a newer, faster bicycle, books, paper,and a pen, which gave me an outlet to write. Like biking it soothes my soul. When I turned eighteen and had to leave the orphanage there was enough money from all the tips to rent a small abode above a fish shop. God had provided a means for my livelihood, and as long as I kept my head and face covered people treated me with some dignity.

Thank you for looking at me with dignity, Elise. God bless you, my angel.

Ludwig

30 August 1914

Dear Elise,

The late summer weather here in eastern Prussia continues to be unbearably hot and humid. Morning coolness is fleeting, and by 8:00 a.m. the sun and humidity suck out any moisture that may be in our bodies. Simple movements like standing have become labor. Water is a commodity that has become more valuable than gold. Men are losing their sanity as they dehydrate. Cordial conversation among members of the 31st is reserved only for our superiors. Instead, we snarl curt comments at each other. Schwarz, in particular, has become a beast. The other day he started a battle over a piece of shade that a lower-ranking soldier had taken over. Only the timely intervention of Captain Lichtwasser prevented an all-out riot. Many people like myself avoid contact with Schwarz at all costs. He is ruthless, but during war time it is a trait that is admired and even coveted by army leaders.

The Russians must also be suffering. Their daily bombings are sporadic. In this incredible heat it takes too much effort to load up the cannons. Our reply to this feeble bombing by the Russians is much the same—one or two blasts here and there. Delivering messages has become almost impossible. Without water, my head spins like a top and I have trouble balancing on my bicycle.

Today, however, there was a welcome respite from this deplorable situation. This morning, on my journey back from the 22nd, I took another route. It brought me through a thick, well-shaded forest that eventually gave way to a lovely little lake. There was only one thing to do. Throwing the messages onto the ground while pedaling, I rode the bicycle straight into the water until it was completely submerged. The coolness of the water was such a relief! It felt like I was falling into the bed of a king. Lapping the water up like a dog, my body rejoiced in its life giving energy. Half an hour swept by before I finally dragged myself and the bicycle out of the lake. After picking up the messages that I had thrown down I rode with sopping wet clothes back to the 31st; it had been a long time since I had felt such happiness and contentment.

My arrival back at the company was met with great interest. Speck ordered half of us to follow me back to the lake, which was about three kilometers away. The other half would go once we had returned.

The joy of the men as they jumped into the water fully clothed was expressed with laughter, whoops, smiles, and blissful relief. Even the cantankerous Schwarz forgot about twisting his face into a scowl and turned his lips up into a small smile.

By the end of the day, every member of the 31st had splashed and been revived in the gentle, cool waters of that little lake. Canteens and any other container that could hold water were filled to the brim. No one shed their clothing; they let them dry right on their bodies. That evening, energized by the lake, we bombed the Russians with great gusto.

Later, Lichtwasser came up to me, smiling widely so that his shiny, white teeth sparkled in the setting sun. "You are a good cyclist, Schmidt. Thank you."

"Yes, sir."

"Good night."

"Yes, sir."

Lichtwasser nodded and strode away. The captain is a great man, and as I settled in for the night I thought about how and why I got to the Eastern Front.

The Germans are badly outnumbered by their enemies and desperately need more men to solidify the lines. Initially I was told that the Kaiser does not take disfigured men for his army. Yet, I can ride a bicycle. I can ride a bicycle faster than any man. So upon the recommendation of Herr Maier, the chocolate shop owner, I was conscripted into the Kaiser's Army and assigned to the 31st Company, a group of 150 men, as a cyclist. The 31st Company's camp was located in the countryside fifteen kilometers east of Lüebeck.

I arrived there early on a beautiful spring morning with some trepidation. People's first reaction to my face is invariably negative. The leaders of the 31st would not change my beliefs about this. At first Speck and the other Kommandants of the 31st were outraged that a man like myself would even get a recommendation to be in the army. In fact, Speck and Schwarz were adamant that I was not fit for service and their voices were filled with outrage as they ridiculed my facial appearance. It was as if the scar tissue covering my forehead and left cheek was all the proof they needed that I was incompetent. It was Lichtwasser who suggested that I at least be given a chance to prove that I was as good a cyclist as Herr Maier claimed. After much heated debate with Lichtwasser, Speck reluctantly agreed to give me an opportunity. He demanded that I race against three able-bodied men to see if I was at least physically able to ride a bicycle. If I won the race I would be allowed to train as a cyclist and soldier with the 31st. If I lost I would be assigned as a server in the base's mess hall.

So, thirty minutes after arriving at the 31st Company's base, I along with three very fit men each got a bicycle. The three aspiring soldiers allegedly knew how to ride a bicycle. Each one of them wanted to beat me and the others in the upcoming race due to Speck's offer of money and extra food rations if they finished first. They took turns looking down at me with a smug sneer and mocking eyes. Then the three men joked about whether one of them should get a children's bicycle for me, since the one I received was rather large compared to my height. *No problem*, I thought, *let them laugh*. Unlike my three competitors I made sure the tires of my bicycle had plenty of air and the chain was well greased. After some delay getting this rectified, I was ready to go. The others could not be bothered to check if their bicycles were roadworthy. Such was their arrogance or more accurately their ignorance of bicycles. I noted that Lichtwasser observed my actions with some respect.

The race was simple. We were to cycle to Lüebeck, buy some beer, and return them to the Kommandants back at base. Speck and the others thought for sure that I would fail. In fact, they gave me the option to not even take the challenge so I could avoid the humiliation of losing. Not a chance. It was clear to me that God had given me the skill, strength, and passion to cycle well. I would race for the Lord and show the others I was more than capable of being a cyclist for the Kaiser's army. I was also grateful to Lichtwasser who had supported me, and I wanted to repay his faith in me with my best effort.

As soon as the race began, my three competitors pedaled furiously, leaving me far behind. From my own personal experience I knew this was a mistake on their part. I pedaled hard but steady and by the ten kilometer mark I had easily passed the huffing and puffing men. Upon entering Lüebeck I quickly found a restaurant selling bottled beer, put them into my rucksack and headed back. I passed my three challengers as they were entering Lüebeck. One of them, upset that I was beating them, tried to catch me with the obvious intention of knocking me over, but with some deft maneuvers I easily got by him. I headed back to base, leaving the three in my wake.

The surprise on the Kommandants' faces was etched clearly when I arrived. Speck was stunned as he muttered, "I don't believe what I am seeing." The Kommandants quietly opened up their beer bottles, took some satisfying swigs of the brew, and waited for the other three men. It was a long wait. I stood at ease for over half an hour until they finally arrived. Speck excused himself earlier, leaving only Lichtwasser and Schwarz to witness the embarrassing return of my three fellow competitors. After harshly reprimanding the three late comers, Schwarz came up to me and haughtily declared, "I am surprised with your effort, yet I can see your skill as a cyclist will be of some use for our company." With that he shuffled off. Lichtwasser grinned thinly and uttered, "Consider that a great compliment from Sergeant Schwarz. He's an excellent soldier, but rather gruff as a person. Be careful not to get on his bad side."

"Yes, sir!" I responded.

Lichtwasser smiled serenely at me and said, "Welcome to the 31st Company, Private Schmidt. I think you will be a good cyclist."

It was not easy training for war. The physical demands were difficult, but worse, the inhumanity shown to me by some of the other recruits was unbearable. Sergeant Anon Schwarz, a tall, dark, muscular man with the eyes of a crow, in particular made it his mission to transform me into a soldier. He was ruthless with his demands that I learn how to handle a rifle. Despite my best efforts I, much to Schwarz's chagrin, only became an average marksman. Schwarz also demanded that I, along with the others, become physically fit. We ran and exercised for hours. Again, much to Schwarz's chagrin, I was only strong and skilled on a bicycle. When it came to running or hand to hand combat I was mediocre at best. One day Schwarz, in obvious disgust with my average abilities as a warrior, pulled my scarf down in front of twenty other soldiers and loudly announced, "What do you think men, is this the face of a brave German soldier? Is it?" There was some cruel laughter and the ugly feelings of humiliation washed over me. The other Kommandants arrived and Schwarz and the others went quiet as I quickly pulled the scarf back over my face. I buried the hurt and rage I felt deep inside me, on to the emotional agony I had collected since the fire.

Kommandant Uli Speck was also mean to me, but he was that way to everyone. His anger towards us was meant to motivate us. This I could, with much reluctance, respect. We were about to enter a war, a very serious life-and-death situation, and the Kommandant wanted us to be completely obedient to him and completely ruthless toward the enemy. This attitude would no doubt give us a decent chance for survival. Kommandant Uli Speck's body has a wide girth due to his fondness for sausages and beer. His size made his demands even more intimidating. However, a soldier's diet may change all that.

The other leader of the 31st is a handsome, tall, blond man named Heribert Lichtwasser. Captain Lichtwasser is very demanding, but fair, and carries himself with great dignity. Every man respects the captain.

Even Sergeant Schwarz smartens up around this man. Still, despite the presence of Lichtwasser, the opportunities for Schwarz to abuse me during training were numerous and he did not forsake them. Often, I wrestled with ugly, ungodly thoughts toward Schwarz. Yet, I sought refuge in the Scriptures, particularly:

Revenge is mine, says the Lord. (Romans 12:19)

Do not be overcome by evil, but overcome evil with good. (Romans 12:21)

At times I longed for God to provide a vicious revenge.

In the evenings, during free time, I rode my bicycle and left the taunts and ugly stares of the 31st wallowing in the dust. That helped a lot. And always, my reading, writing, and dreams of you have given me pleasant thoughts. So Elise, I believe you are an angel, sent by God to give me some hope. I will write letters to you, but I will never send them because of fear. Fear that you are not what I believe, fear that you will be like everyone else and reject me. No. You are like an angel. You are hope. I need hope.

The thought of you rejecting my love is too unbearable to contemplate. Maybe someday I will have the courage to approach you with my heart held out. Maybe you will be able to see past my ugly shell. God, I am so frail!   Forgive me, my angel.

Ludwig

12 September 1914

Dear Elise,

The hot, humid conditions that nearly drained all the life out of us a few weeks ago are thankfully over. The weather is getting noticeably cooler and there has been nothing but rain, rain, rain, rain, rain. I have been drenched to the bone, seemingly forever. We are constantly on maneuvers—day, night, it doesn't matter. It is all a diversionary tactic to fool the Russians into believing that there are thousands of us, that to attack us would be foolhardy. Judging by the skirmishes, the dead Russians we find, reports from spies, and the thousands of prisoners we take in, our enemy from the east must outnumber us at least five to one. The Kaiser needs to send more troops, but the Western Front requires soldiers too. As a result new recruits are few and far between. Some parts of the front line are paper thin, so we march to those points, dig some trenches, roll out barbed wire, and blast a few salvos towards the enemy. It's all a ruse to show strength and power. We are so weak at some spots on the front that the war would probably be over in two days if the Russians attacked them. If only they knew. So we march and march. Pretending. Many soldiers lose their boots in the mud and end up trudging in their socks. Some men fall by the wayside or get lost, especially at night, and some don't catch up with us for a week or two.

I've got a cold; others are sick with pneumonia, flu, bronchitis; the hacking and coughing amongst the soldiers is incessant. Food is whatever we can scrape up from an abandoned farm or village. Farm animals such as chickens or cows are quickly slaughtered for soup. My bicycle is rather useless now—too many roads here are nothing but mud bogs. So I carry it. Rain, rain, rain, rain, when will it end?

This morning, long before the sun's arrival would turn the heavy black clouds to gray, I was awakened by Schwarz.

"Schmidt, get up!"

I stirred.

"Get up!"

I lifted my head and opened my eyes.

"Kommandant Speck needs these orders to be delivered to Kommandant Heinrich! Now!"

I stood up, saluted, and uttered. "Yes, sir."

"What? Speak up!"

"Yes, sir."

"Not good enough! What?"

"Yes, sir."

Speck, roused by the commotion, bellowed from his trench. "Shut up, Schwarz! Let the fool go! Disturb my sleep again and you will be bringing that order!"

Schwarz glared at me and hissed, "You are not a warrior. I don't want to fight or die for you. I don't believe you are capable of fighting for me. You are only a decent cyclist. You ever stop being that I will...." Schwarz raised a clenched fist and then slinked away. *Forgive Him, Father, for he does not know what he is doing.* Luke 23:34

I prayed and pushed my bicycle hard through the muck, and soon Schwarz's abuse washed away. I entered a forest that was so dark I couldn't see my hands. There was a sudden crack of thunder and rain, like a waterfall, fell on me. The muck became so thick on the bicycle's tires that I had to lug it on my back. I also had to be careful not to lose my boots in the sticky ooze that enveloped them with every step. I trudged forward slower than a turtle. The only sounds were rain, my steps, and my slow breathing. The only thing I could see was black. Finally, after what seemed like hours, my absurd situation ceased. The rain stopped and I came out of the mud onto what felt like a meadow. I was so exhausted I collapsed onto the sopping, wet ground. I lay there for several minutes still blinded by the black night. Suddenly, adrenaline kicked through my body. A voice?

I rasped the password, "Hummel, hummel."

Silence. Why did I not hear the response, "Murs, murs"?

Again I heard something.

I spoke as loud as I could, "Hummel, hummel."

The blast of a gun followed by the distinct sounds of the Russian language flew over my head. I remained prone.

A candle was lit only a few meters from where I lay. Thankfully, its illumination was minute in the heavy darkness. Three, four, or maybe even ten Russian voices cut through the air. They sounded anxious. I remained on the ground, still and quiet as death. The candlelight was coming toward me.

Boom!

Thunder crashed, releasing a violent downpour of rain that snuffed the candle instantly. I heard irritated Russian voices. The voices were coming closer, and then abruptly they faded away.

I heard nothing but rain for at least fifteen minutes. Eventually it slowed to a drizzle and finally, mercifully, nothing. The black turned to gray as the sun tried to make its daily entrance. I looked around. I was lying in a gray meadow with gray trees surrounding it. That was all. I got up gingerly, picked up the bicycle and pushed it along with every sense in my body on high alert.

Eventually I found a road. There was a gravel edge that felt like gold as my bicycle got traction. With the caked mud from the tires flying on and over my body I headed in a direction that I thought was correct. With the sun hidden behind a cloud, I was, truthfully, very, very lost. I pedaled on. Suddenly, the sun evaporated and a bank of black clouds appeared. My stressed mind fiddled over the fact—sun comes up in the east, which is where the Russians are, that is bad. The opposite side, toward the dark, is the west, which is good. With some relief I realized that I had chosen the correct direction from the meadow. The distinct sounds of German cannons sending their "good morning payload" over to the Russians gave me more relief. I was not that far from the front.

The sun fought through some more clouds and was actually feeling vaguely warm when I discovered Kommandant Heinrich and other members of his company entrenched in a shallow ditch. I relayed the information to him that during the deep, morning darkness I had overshot his position and I had inadvertently entered Russian territory. This dramatic realization left me in a befuddled state as I stood before the Kommandant.

Heinrich looked exhausted, depressed, and angry all at once. Half of his unit had died the day before and another quarter had been wounded protecting their position. I gave Heinrich the order. He read it grimly. Then he demanded that I take off the scarf around my face. He also made me take off the glasses and hat. The Kommandant laughed grimly when he saw my full face. Then he hissed, "Put it back on, put it all back on now! That's an order! Of course I would receive this message, that will destroy us all, from an angel of death! Now write this down. We are outnumbered at least ten to one. We are going to die today if we don't get reinforcements! Get help, before we all go to hell!"

I got on my bicycle.

It took me three hours to return back to Speck. He took the message, read it, and crumpled it in disgust. "Stupid Heinrich," he muttered. "There is no way we can help him. The Russians could stroll all the way to Berlin if we left our post." Speck looked up at me and shook his head. He grunted, "Get out of here, cyclist. Get some rest."

I crawled into a trench, pulled straw around my cold body and started writing to you.

Thank you, my angel, for hope. There is little of that here at present.

Ludwig

18 September 1914

Dear Elise,

Today was the "Great Day," although it did not start out with much promise. Speck roused me early to bring a message to the 22nd. It was raining as usual, and the roads and trails had been transformed into muddy rivers, which meant I had to carry the bicycle for at least half the trip. Finally, after three hours, I reached the 22nd; they, in turn, loaded me down with a heavy sack full of mail and packages for the 31st. The sack was awkward and heavy, yet I knew there would be joy at the end of my journey. The 31st hadn't received mail in weeks and the men were getting rather aggravated from the lack of news from home. Mercifully, the rain let up and the sun came out quickly drying the edges of the trail. Those edges allowed me to travel more steadily and I was back to the 31st in an hour and a half.

News of my arrival with a sack full of correspondence swept through the group and I was soon engulfed with soldiers eager for their portion. Lichtwasser calmly and firmly took command of handing out the letters and parcels. Most of the men opened what they had received immediately and several wept openly after they had read the messages from their loved ones. Only Schwarz, like I had noticed before during mail times, did not open the one letter he received. Instead he twirled it slowly in his hand for a few seconds and then abruptly, with one swift motion, tore the letter in half, crumpled it up, and threw it into one of the giant mud puddles nearby. With his head down he stomped off back to his station.

Lichtwasser, loaded down with several packages and letters, came up to me and asked, "No mail for you today, Schmidt?"

"No, sir."

"Sorry, I did not hear what you said. Take that scarf off so I can hear you better." With great reluctance I slowly took off the scarf. Lichtwasser repeated his question. "No mail for you today, Schmidt?"

"No, sir."

"I have noticed that you write a letter every night. To whom? Surely it is time that they write back to you, correct?"

"Yes, sir."

Lichtwasser paused and looked down at me with a small grin. "*She,* and I assume it is a *she,* must be important."

"Pardon me, sir?"

"The one you write to every night. *She* is a *she,* yes?"

"Yes, sir."

"I also assume that *she* is a beauty."

"Yes, sir. *She* is an angel."

Lichtwasser laughed out loud. "*She* must be an extraordinary angel to have a man write to her every night."

"Yes, sir."

Lichtwasser laughed again and reached out a small package to me. "Here Schmidt, take this."

"No, I could not do that, sir."

"Why not? I insist. You were a good cyclist today. Look at all these bawling babies around us. Besides, I've got a lot. I'm sure old Aunt Paula would understand if I passed this package on to you."

"No, sir. Please."

"That's enough, Schmidt. Take this package from my aunt. That is an order!"

Reluctantly I consented. Lichtwasser wasn't through, however. He turned to the men around him and bellowed. "Listen everyone! The cyclist didn't receive anything from his angel today, but he did bring happiness to the rest of us! How about we all give a small token from our treasures to the cyclist? He is the bearer of good news!"

Such was the regard for Lichtwasser that every man who received a package from home that day consented to the captain's request and handed me something. Chocolate, coffee, candy, razors, cigarettes, cigars, canned sardines, and more. It was incredible. There was so much that I had to use the mail sack to carry everything back to my sleeping area. Very carefully I opened Aunt Paula's package first. There was a letter included, which I saved for Lichtwasser. The rest was a variety of grooming items such as a comb, little mirror, razor, soap, and hand towel. Thank you, old Aunt Paula.

That night a few men invited me to the evening fire where I was asked to tell them about you, my angel. Before I was allowed to speak though, Captain Lichtwasser ordered me to remove the scarf and dark glasses from my face. In fact he proclaimed to everyone that from now on I was not allowed to wear the scarf or dark glasses around any of the 31st.

This order overwhelmed me. The scarf and glasses had been my shield against the ugly stares and taunts of people for the last several years. Taking them off made me feel naked and ashamed. I slowly and reluctantly pulled them off. There was a long awkward silence as I braced myself for the usual horrifying response that people have when they see my face. Not tonight. The response of all the men, when they saw my face illuminated brightly by the roaring fire, was...indifference. *Indifference.* Indifference to the horror of my face. Speck with a hint of irritation said, "Well, cyclist? Come on, speak up! Tell us about the angel!"

I stuttered a bit at first, but once I started describing you my words became smooth and eloquent. I spoke about your eyes, the ones that transmit peace, grace, and sweetness. I spoke about your voice and its gentle, soothing melody. I spoke about your patience and the ready smile you have when relating to people. I spoke about your lovely hair and your breathtaking figure. When I finished, there was a long pause. The men sat silently, grinning at me. The interlude was finally broken when a soldier said with a forlorn tone, "I think I am in love."

This comment received a loud round of laughter. I could only nod shyly. This was greeted with more laughter and then it was on to another story. Later that night as the fire died and it was time to sleep, I stepped up to Lichtwasser, gave him his letter from Aunt Paula, and said, "Thank you, sir."

"For what?"

"For treating me like a man."

"You are a great man. Never forget that."

"Your aunt sent you...er, me a grooming kit."

"Good old Aunt Paula. She sends me grooming kits all the time. The kit you have would have been my fifth."

Smiling, while rubbing his gruff, unshaven face, Lichtwasser asked, "Seriously, Schmidt, do you really think I need another grooming kit?"

"No, sir, you look just fine."

"Thank you, Schmidt, I agree with your assessment. Aunt Paula is a little senile, but her heart is sound. You have a good sleep, Schmidt. Say hello from me to your angel."

"Yes, sir. Good night."

I slept, despite the rain, cold, and discomfort, blissfully.

It was the greatest day of my adult life. Thank you, Elise, for being my angel.

Ludwig

28 September 1914

Dear Elise,

The respect and dignity I received from Lichtwasser and others of the 31st on the *Great Day* has not stopped. Every day since then, "my comrades" have smiled at me, said hello, invited me into their conversation, and so on. It is still hard for me to grasp that the scarf and glasses, which covered my face for so many years and were part of my identity for much too long, have been ordered off. And no one seems to *care*! I am overwhelmed with this kindness. I am like a man who, after subsisting on dry bread crusts and water for years, is suddenly invited to a royal feast. How do you respond? Where do you begin?

The post has started to find its way to the 31st with more regularity and it is now deemed good luck to give the cyclist (yours truly) a token for bringing correspondence from the Fatherland. It amazes me how one man, Lichtwasser, has changed almost a whole company's perspective.

I say almost because Sergeant Schwarz's conflicted stance toward me remains. He respects my cycling abilities, but my courage and skills as a soldier absolutely not. I hate him for that because I would lay my life down for my comrades. My disdain for the sergeant and his character and stance against me runs deep. For now only prayer, scripture, and riding hard on my bicycle gives me some relief from the tension of hate I have toward Schwarz.

Until today.

The day started out beautiful. The sun, after a week-long hiatus behind a raincloud, reappeared. The Russians for some reason didn't send their usual morning thunder. Maybe the sunny day made them forget. Speck decided to withhold his order for our usual return reply. It was all warm, light, and quiet on the Eastern Front.

The happiness I felt was shared by many. Lots of smiles and laughter lit up the 31st Company. There was peace in my step that morning as I moved along in the trenches, looking for Lichtwasser and my orders for the day. I came upon a section of the trenches that was deserted, or at least I thought so. Schwarz suddenly, seemingly out of nowhere, came down a ladder and stepped in front of me, forcing me to brake. He stared down at me in silent disdain. I tried to move around him. He moved and blocked the way. I tried again. He moved and blocked the way. Then he snarled, "Your mother was a whore!" Then he pushed me down and walked off.

Despite my commitment to God, despite my efforts to feel compassion, despite my efforts to constantly forgive, ride, and talk the pain away, the trauma of this latest abuse was too much for me. As I lay there in the dirt panting in anger, humiliation, and shock, my mind hurtled over an edge into a black abyss. Schwarz had gone too far; he had gone too far for much too long. No! Not my mother! Not my dead mother! Her love gave me life! Her love is still giving me life! No one, but no one, especially Sergeant Schwarz, had the right to defame my mother! So what if he is hurting and taking his hurt out on me! That was no excuse! To hell with him! *Do not murder.* God? Where are You? I was not going to listen to Him anyway! My mind was long gone from Him! *Do not murder.*

My dear angel Elise, I confess that I found a rifle and pulled off its bayonet. Then I concealed it up the right sleeve of my coat. Sergeant Schwarz had not walked far from his crime against me. He was alone, sitting down on a wooden box, and focused on cleaning some boots. He did not notice my arrival. *Do not murder.* I let the bayonet slide into my hand. *Do not murder.* Schwarz had gone too far! *Do not murder.* My mind was reeling with rage. Deadly rage. *Do not murder!*

"Schmidt!"

Captain Lichtwasser called out my name and it felt like a slap across the face. It was that startling. My heart pounded in shock, but I found enough composure to slide the bayonet back up the sleeve.

"Schmidt!"

"Yes, sir!"

The captain ordered me to deliver a message to the 54th Company. Right away. Schwarz looked up from the boots. When he saw me his lips curled into a mocking smile. Then he looked into my eyes. They were deadly. His smile faded.

I rode hard on a German bicycle—my English one was getting its tire fixed—and cried profusely, yelled Scripture, but the usual relief did not come this time. After two hours I arrived at the 54th's position, my mind still slithering in darkness. The 54th had survived a hard Russian attack in the early morning hours. The Kommandant was concerned that the line had been breached. "Careful," he warned. "I sent a few patrols to assess the situation, but there could be Russians who have managed to get through and are on maneuvers to outflank German positions."

I listened to this with some skepticism. The Russians were incompetent and disorganized. At least, that is what our German military leaders had trained us to believe. Returning back to the 31st I came upon a fork in the road. The trail to the right skirted the front by a wide margin and was the safer choice. It was the right choice. It was the trail I had initially come from. According to my map, the left trail was dangerous and led to the front. Dark thoughts overwhelmed me. Go right and live another day with Schwarz, go left and possibly die. At least then I would be free from his torment. What was my life with the sergeant? Misery. I went left.

For several kilometers it was serene. The birds twittered amongst the trees. There was a gentle breeze that fluttered the leaves like tiny flags. The sky was baby blue adorned with white, pillow-like clouds. The darkness in my head started giving way to light.

I have created you to do good works in Christ Jesus. (Ephesians 2:10)

Do not be overcome by evil, but overcome evil with good. (Romans 12:21)

A very large and very steep hill came into view. Getting off my bicycle at the base, I took a swig of water from my canteen and glanced at the map. Only three kilometers to the 31st. Until this hill the trail had been delightful. Much more scenic than the one I had come on. The hill was too steep to ride up so I started pushing the bike to its crest. More light entered the dark corners of my mind: *Consider it pure joy when trials come at you from all sides. Consider it pure joy what Schwarz is doing. Faith. Faith will give you perspective on what is really important. Schwarz's words are not important. Jesus suffered and died for you. Now that is most important. It is everything.*

Eventually I arrived at the top of the hill. This brief journey had been good. My head was filled with light. Life on God's terms. That was what made it worthwhile. Boarding the bicycle with renewed vigor, I exulted in what lay before me—a long, gently sloping trail through a meadow into another forest about a kilometer away. Thrilled by the momentum that the hill provided my bicycle, I pedaled furiously and was moving at a tremendous clip when I entered the forest. The speed saved my life.

Russians. Their uniforms were unmistakable. Several of them. At least a hundred. They were walking single file along the edge of the trail, heading straight towards the 31st. The bicycle, with me crouched as low as possible on it, flew noiselessly by them. Cries of surprise, Russian cries of surprise, when they saw me, hit my ears as my legs pumped furiously like overheated pistons. Some of the Russians turned into the trail, but I wasn't stopping. They either scrambled for dear life at the last possible second or were painfully clipped by one of my elbows and sent sprawling into the brush. Despite the advantages of incredible speed and the element of surprise, there seemed to be no end to the Russians. They yelled at me in startled or agitated voices. Finally I came around a corner and was almost clear of the enemy.

Bang. Bang.

Bullets clanged through my bicycle's back wheel, obliterating several spokes. The wheel, now severely weakened, started to bend due to my weight and the jarring terrain of the trail. This caused the bicycle to wobble severely underneath me and added to the terror I was feeling. I was tempted to stop and get off the wildly careening bicycle, but a bullet whistled by my left ear. Either a bullet or a bicycle crash was going to kill me. I decided the bicycle crash would be better. Being shot at reinvigorated my legs with another rush of adrenaline. They were a blur as I pumped the pedals. Another volley of bullets flew beside me. They crashed into some nearby trees with a sickening thud. A sharp right on the trail, a downturn into a small valley, and I was out of sight and range of the Russians. The shooting had ended, but the fantastic speed of my wobbling bicycle had not. Now absolutely out of control and hanging on to it with everything that was in me, I whistled into a clearing and there, praise the Lord, was the 31st. Most of them were lounging in the sun. Some were playing cards; others were talking; a few were reading. Two or three looked up and saw me coming. Bam! The bicycle's back wheel collapsed, causing me to spin out of control. Mercifully there was plenty of tall, soft grass to brace the head over heels flight I took off the bicycle. Those who witnessed this spectacular crash laughed uproariously. For several minutes I lay there, wind knocked out of me, too stunned to move. Finally, Lichtwasser came up with a few other men.

"Schmidt? Speak to me. Are you alright?"

Breathing was difficult, but I whispered, "Russians."

"What?"

"Russians. There must be a hundred of them. They are outflanking us. They are coming through the woods."

It took a moment for Lichtwasser's brain to register what I had said. Then his eyes opened up in terror. "Alarm! Russians advancing towards us from behind!

The 31st scurried hard to battle stations. Cannons were wheeled around. Machine guns were set up. It took barely two minutes for everything to be ready. Struggling to my feet I limped over to a trench and collapsed into it. It was quiet. Only a gentle breeze fluttering the leaves of the nearby forest could be heard. After several minutes of this Lichtwasser finally whispered, "Well Schmidt, where are they?"

The words were barely out of his mouth when a bullet whipped over the trench. The Russians attacked, screaming their distinct war cry. Our cannons thundered a reply, obliterating many of the attackers. The machine guns mowed down several more. The battle was short, but grisly. The Russians who survived this savage retort by the 31st raised their arms in surrender. Final tally was 37 dead Russians and 45 prisoners. The 31st lost four. A few Russians had managed to escape back into the forest, but it was still an impressive victory for the 31st.

Lichtwasser found me later in the evening, huddled in my straw nest, writing to you, Elise. He was carrying a map, which piqued my curiosity. Due to my tumble off the bicycle I was extremely stiff, which made standing up difficult, but eventually I managed that and a sharp salute as well. The captain smiled and said, "Writing to your angel?"

"Yes, sir."

"Well, you certainly have lots to write about after a day like this one."

"Yes, sir."

"I don't mean to keep you from corresponding with your angel, but why did you return down the eastern trail? According to this map, the western trail skirted the front by a wide margin while the eastern one is practically in enemy territory."

"The reason is personal," I stammered.

"Personal?"

"Yes, sir."

"Schmidt, in the future, your decisions must be based on what serves the company best. Choosing a dangerous route when you could have taken a safer one is not acceptable. Do I make myself clear?"

"Yes, sir."

"Although you saved our lives today you took an enormous and unnecessary risk." Lichtwasser looked into my eyes and continued, "You are a good cyclist, Schmidt. The 31$_{st}$ can ill afford to lose someone as valuable as you."

"Yes, sir."

"Furthermore, I consider you a friend," Lichtwasser stretched out his hand. We shook hands and the captain said, "I don't want to lose you."

"Yes, sir."

Lichtwasser grinned at this and started walking off. Suddenly he turned around and said, "Oh, I almost forgot. I've nominated you for an Iron Cross. Your actions today were exemplary. Congratulations."

"Thank you, sir."

"My pleasure. Make sure you let your angel know about your nomination. Good night."

"Yes, sir. Good night, sir."

Thus ended the most remarkable day of my life. Elise, it was providence that Lichtwasser came as the bayonet slid into my hand. It was providence that I found the Russians. I was wrong for wanting to kill a fellow human being, a creature created by the same God who made me. It was wrong for me to tempt fate and do something that could have gotten me killed. Please forgive me, Angel. I promise to treasure life, no matter what Schwarz says, and with God's help I'll treasure his. I will also treasure mine. Today a man said he valued me as a friend. That is a miracle, my angel. I have found a place where I belong. It is the 31st Company of Kaiser Wilhelm's army. God bless us all. Thank you, Angel, for smiling at me. Sweet dreams.

Ludwig

10 October 1914

Dear Elise,

Despite God's grace, which saved me from murdering Schwarz; despite my proclamations and prayers to see him through the eyes of Jesus; despite all that, my hate for the sergeant gnaws at my soul. While I did not murder Sergeant Schwarz in the flesh, I have murdered him in my heart. God has made it very clear through His Spirit and Scripture that this is sin. Knowing that my mother and father would be devastated with the state of my heart toward Schwarz has also been extremely painful to ponder. The thought, *If I wasn't so different, Schwarz would respect me,* has also rattled around in my head. For many days God has seemed far away as I have wrestled with my deep offense toward the sergeant and the Lord's insistence that I let it go.

Receiving the Iron Cross should have been one of the greatest moments in my life. It was, but later I suffered. The kommandants had us gather together in front of a small podium. Speck stood on it first and blustered about me destroying a fine German bicycle. Thankfully my English one was ready for service again. Speck and the others were still blissfully ignorant of the nationality of my favorite bicycle and would be forevermore. Lichtwasser, all smiles as usual, reminded everyone that I was a man to be respected. As I came up to the captain to receive the Iron Cross, I gazed at the faces of the 31st. All were smiling except Sergeant Schwarz. His eyes burned with disgust. Lichtwasser pinned the great German honor on my chest and the men cheered. Feelings of euphoria and gratitude lightened my body.

The happiness lasted until that evening when I walked to my place of rest—a shabby tool shed in a battle-scarred farmyard. I was about to enter it when Sergeant Schwarz emerged out of the darkness without warning. The light from a raging bonfire nearby flickered off our faces. We stared at each other, expressionless, for several seconds. Only our eyes betrayed deep hurt and anger. Then Schwarz abruptly turned and disappeared into the darkness.

With that I tramped into the shed, covered myself in straw, and wrote to you. Sergeant Schwarz brings my faith to an edge. How and why do I trust God? How important is He to me? Is the sacrifice of Jesus Christ sufficient for me to do things the way God wants? Do I desire God's comfort and counsel in every situation that I encounter? Can I understand that God created Schwarz? Can I abide by: *Do not be overcome by evil, but overcome evil with good?*

11 October 1914

Dear Elise,

Praise be to the God and Father of our Lord Jesus Christ! In his great mercy he has given us new birth into a living hope through the resurrection of Jesus Christ from the dead, into an inheritance that can never perish, spoil or fade—kept in heaven for you, who through faith are shielded by God's power until the coming of the salvation that is ready to be revealed in the last time. In this you greatly rejoice, though now for a little while you may have had to suffer grief in all kinds of trials. These have come so that your faith—of greater worth than gold, which perishes even though refined by fire—may be proved genuine and may result in praise, glory, and honor when Jesus Christ is revealed (1 Peter 1:3-7).

My faith is under a great trial. After spending the night in anguished prayer, it was clear what I was supposed to do the next morning. Captain Lichtwasser listened to my comments about how Schwarz always throws away his one letter with some interest. He patted me on the shoulder and said, "You are a good cyclist, but more importantly, you are a good man, Schmidt. This must be the hundredth time I've told you so. But there is a war on and I can't concern myself too much with a soldier's personal life."

"Yes, sir."

"Is there anything else?"

"No, sir."

"How has Schwarz been treating you lately?"

"Fine, sir."

"Fine?"

"Yes, sir."

With a sarcastic tone, Lichtwasser declared, "From what I have observed, Schwarz does seem to have a warm place for you in his heart."

"He seems to be that way with mostly everyone."

"Indeed. You are a man, Schmidt. A good man. I trust you will continue to deal with Schwarz in an appropriate fashion."

"Yes, sir."

"By the way, upon my recommendation Kommandant Speck assigned Sergeant Schwarz to permanent patrol duty. He is an excellent spy and runs his little unit top class."

"Yes, sir."

"So Schwarz will not be around us much, which I think is just as well. Now here are your orders. A message needs to be delivered to the 77th immediately."

"Yes, sir."

So that is it, Angel. God has answered my prayer and obviously those of many others. There was a calm over the 31st today. Schwarz and his little unit were on patrol and away from us. The war with its constant cold, wet, hunger, pain, and despair is nothing for me when I consider the evil of Sergeant Schwarz. Standing up to him in the name of Jesus has been a major step for me in becoming a man. Now that the sergeant is on patrol it will give us all a respite from his simmering cruelty. Thank God. I am thankful that I have you, my dear angel, to share my deepest fears and triumphs with.

Ludwig

25 October 1914

Dear Elise,

Sergeant Schwarz and his patrol gear up early every morning for their missions. They often make dangerous forays into enemy territory, but they always return. So far. Occasionally I have seen Schwarz, but he always seems too preoccupied with his thoughts to notice anyone. Once I saw him with a letter. He looked at it for a long time and then, as usual, he ripped it in two and sent the pieces flying into a fire. It is such a mystery to me. Why does he keep doing that? God knows.

Outside of Schwarz there is much to be thankful about. Lichtwasser and many others in the company still continue to show positive interest in my life. It is tonic to my bones. I am so grateful and have learned how to reciprocate. Most men have pictures of their family and are very happy to show them to me, which I allow. I also endure a character description of each member. For once I am happy that my facial muscles cannot express boredom; I just hope my eyes don't betray me. Yet the appearance of interest in my comrade's families makes them glad and builds affection and trust between us.

This affection is most evident at post delivery time when Lichtwasser and several others give me something from their packages. Invariably they ask about you, Angel. "Why doesn't she write?" they question. I tell them you touch my heart every time I say your name so I do not need your words. The men shake their heads, smile with amusement, and tell me I am crazy. Then they drift off into another conversation or duty.

While post delivery at the 31st is a moment of joy for most men, the weather lately has turned cold and wet. As a result, our morale is sinking.

The drudgery of the war is also starting to sap the life out of us. We are descending into a place where we just exist. Eat, sleep, do our duty, eat, sleep, do our duty. The moments when we live—laugh, cry, smile, frown, converse, share, have fun—rarely happen. It is all gray, gray, cold, wet, gray, wet, and cold, with the Russians bringing flashes of terror that leave some of us wounded, some of us dead, and the rest of us shattered.

As for myself, I must travel at least fifty to one hundred kilometers every day, transferring orders, mail, and whatever foodstuffs I can buy for my company. When I have the good fortune to find a store the selection is meager at best, but the store owners certainly appreciate any money that I give them. And I always have some money from the company. The fifteen marks I receive every month would not go a long way, especially in a war zone where things are scarce. If I cannot find a store then I look for a farm. Often they are abandoned, but I always seem to find a chicken or a bag of potatoes that will be gratefully devoured by the soldiers. I leave some money behind for the things that I take. That is only right. The food I procure is certainly not enough to keep any weight on. We are losing lots of it. Even Speck has lost some puffiness in his cheeks.

Today a little life came into our drab gray lives. However, I wouldn't recommend this "little life" to anyone. Last night the sleeping quarters for the 31st was a castle only 150 meters from the front line. We found several mattresses and after months of straw and mud, laying on them was paradise. This paradise didn't last very long. On the third day of our stay I was ordered by Lichtwasser to report to Speck. I entered the immense boardroom of the castle and presented myself to him. Speck passed an order to me and as he was about to speak, a Russian bomb, at least eighty-five kilos, came crashing through the bay window of the room and landed on a sofa. Speck and I were incredulous as we stared at that instrument of death, laying there comfortably on a soft cushion. We scrambled out of the room, yelling at the top of our lungs. This saved the lives of many. For shortly thereafter, operational bombs, ones that actually worked, hailed onto and into the castle. We all made it to the trenches. But barely. Artillery fire was returned. Massive explosions rocked the earth. Then, as suddenly as it had started, the firing ceased. We looked back at our sleeping quarters. The castle had been reduced to a giant pile of debris. Speck spoke to no one in particular, "Just as well. The mattress was a little hard on my back. Mud and straw will suit me fine tonight."

Good night, my angel, Elise.

Ludwig

27 October 1914

Dear Elise,

It is difficult to remain sane in this war. Today I rode into a destroyed East Prussian town looking to give a message to a man named Kommandant Meyer. It was disturbing to see buildings ruined, horse carcasses lying everywhere, and no civilians. The only signs of life were two German officers sitting in front of a ruined café. They had found several bottles of wine and judging by the smashed bottles at their feet had consumed most of them. With some trepidation I rode up to the officers, got off my bicycle, and provided them with a smart salute. They looked at me with some scorn.

"Who are you, what do you want, and why are you wearing a scarf over your face?" mumbled the elder drunk officer with some difficulty.

"Private Schmidt, 31st Company, bicycle brigade. I have a message for Kommandant Meyer."

The younger officer, a redhead with round spectacles, stirred his lanky body and slurred loudly, "I am Kommandant Meyer. You didn't answer Kommandant Braun's question. Why are you wearing that scarf?"

"Recovering from war wounds," I lied.

"War wounds?" bellowed Braun. "War wounds? Well it is good to see that despite war wounds you are still doing your duties!"

"Thank you sir," I crisply declared, "I have a message for you, sir."

"A message! Unless it says I can go home immediately, I don't want it!" yelled Meyer. Both the kommandants laughed wildly at this comment.

Ignoring his outrageous comments, I held out the message to him. Meyer burped, then snatched it from me. He read it out loud in a mocking tone. "Kommandant Meyer, you and your company are to report at once to the 31st Company and reinforce their position!"

Meyer and Braun burst out laughing. When they had settled down somewhat Meyer retched violently before saying with great disgust, "Who do I take to the 31st? Half of my soldiers are sick, wounded, or dead. The other half is exhausted from fighting those beasts from the east. They are all fast asleep and will probably kill you if they had to get up now. In fact, they might kill us all if we command them to march to the 31st."

"It is an order, sir," I meekly replied.

"What!" screamed Meyer. "Go away, cyclist. My men are three days away from being fit for duty. You tell your kommandant that they are on the march and will arrive in a few days' time. That is an order. Now get on that bicycle and pedal out of here!"

The last thing I heard from that horrible village was Meyer and Braun singing, "The world is getting nicer every day...!"

Later, I relayed the information Meyer had ordered me to say to Speck. He rolled his head from side to side and muttered, "This war is insane. Why are we fighting and dying when there is no hope of victory? We are on two fronts and badly outnumbered. It is all madness!"

I walked away as Speck continued to mutter to himself.

Good night, Elise.

Ludwig

5 November 1914

Dear Elise,

We have advanced into Russia because for some inexplicable reason the Russians, who tormented us for months, have abandoned their trenches. Schwarz has reported that they are moving briskly to the east. The Eastern front is constantly moving back and forth due to its great length (1600 km.) No doubt the Russians are moving back to collect more reinforcements and weapons to forge another assault to the west. So we follow at a safe distance. Entering Russia from East Prussia was like going back in time. The roads are dusty and narrow. The buildings are simple and rustic; the civilians are poorly dressed; many wander around barefoot. The train tracks in Russia are too wide for German trains. No problem. A large work crew manned with crowbars, hammers, and long nails quickly dismantled the tracks and built them to German specifications. Within two days the Kaiser's trains were chugging along, bringing troops and supplies into Russia.

Today we came upon a village that was going up in flames. Schwarz reported that a well-equipped German unit had swept through earlier in the day and engaged the enemy in a short but ruthless battle. Debris, corpses, and horse carcasses lay everywhere. A Russian mother, half out of her mind, came running up to us carrying a baby that could not have been more than a year old. The baby was dead. She screamed at us in a language we could not understand. Yet, the grief and anger she exhibited was clear to us. We passed by silently.

The sun was setting as we came upon a ragged, deserted farm. There were a few lean chickens scrounging for food; they were quickly caught, beheaded, plucked, butchered, and thrown into a soup.

It was pitch black when I staggered into a tiny shed for the night. I slept deeply because the march that day had been long and arduous. The next morning's light illuminated my sleeping quarters and, much to my horror, a dead Russian soldier. His death had obviously been recent since there was minimal decay, yet the sight of his pasty white face, frozen with eyes and mouth open, gave me a fright.

Lichtwasser, upon seeing the corpse, murmured, "Well, at least you weren't disturbed by any snoring last night." The captain and I dragged the deceased and very stiff Russian out of the shed and, with a few others, immediately set about digging a final resting place for him. It was backbreaking work because of the rocky soil. Lichtwasser thanked the Lord out loud when we finally dug a deep enough hole for the corpse. After rolling the dead Russian into it we quickly shoveled dirt over top and then went on with other duties. How many times have we buried dead soldiers from either side? Countless. Our hearts have stiffened as a result. Death is a daily occurrence. It has become so normal to most of us that it barely registers as shocking or awful any more.

After a cup of coffee we marched eastward. Soon we heard the familiar thunder of artillery and Speck ordered me to cycle ahead and let the front line soldiers know we were close at hand. Within fifteen minutes I had arrived. After quickly putting on my scarf and glasses I presented myself to Kommandant Wizenhut. He looked quizzically at my attire, but was too exhausted to care why. He received my news with relief.

I raced back to my unit and Speck listened to the report with some discouragement. "The German Empire is going to lose this war, you know. It is elementary. We're on too many fronts. The only reason we are even still fighting them is that the Russians lack organization! God help us when they do figure things out."

I nodded and thought, *Why are we even in this war?*

I spent the rest of the day near the front, riding hard on my bicycle, informing my superiors of our troop positions and status. By late afternoon several other companies had reached our position. Schwarz and his patrol noted that although there were a great number of Russian soldiers nearby, they were not prepared for battle.

Shortly thereafter the orders came through. Attack! It was well coordinated and the disorganized Russians were easily overwhelmed. One thousand prisoners; four hundred Russians killed; several pieces of military hardware taken and now in the service of the German army. We were all giddy with success.

Just as the sun made its final descent things got even better. A lonely old cow wandering aimlessly on the road was discovered by your faithful cyclist. Within minutes I reported my finding to Speck who promptly enlisted a small unit of men. They followed me with a cart to where I had first spotted the cow. She had not moved much since I had last seen her. In short order it was shot in the head, sawed into pieces, and carted back to the 31st who, in anticipation of a grand meal, had a raging fire ready for barbecuing. Potatoes were also found. It was steak and potatoes for the victors. Amazing how quickly food can be prepared and consumed when there are a lot of hungry men. The feast carried on well into the morning hours. After checking my shed thoroughly with a lit flashlight for unwanted guests, I wrote to you.

Sweet dreams, my angel.

Ludwig

1 December 1914

Dear Elise,

Over the last three weeks we have marched back and forth from Prussia to Russia. The pattern of marching for a few days, then fighting in hastily made trenches for a few days, then pressing forward for a few days before having to head back to fight from old trenches again is numbingly constant. Today we marched eastward and came across several Russian peasants fleeing from their ravaged village. What a pathetic sight.

Women and children, plus very old men were pulling rickety ox carts piled high with what was left of their earthly possessions. An elderly man, wrinkled and stooped by years of labor on the land, stopped Lichtwasser by uttering a few German words to him. Despite the cold weather the aged man's clothes were literally rags hung on a body of protruding bones. He had no shoes; the soles of his feet were rock hard calluses.

The ancient man wailed at Lichtwasser that the eastward moving Russian army had looted and pillaged his village. "Why would our own countrymen do such a thing?" he gasped bitterly through some tears. "Where are we to go?"

The only thing Lichtwasser could think of was to hug him. As he let him go, his cheeks were stained with tears.

Within two hours we entered the still burning village of the old man. Speck, Schwarz, and Lichtwasser became noticeably nervous. It was too quiet. Much too quiet. Speck signaled with his hands for us to go on defensive maneuvers. The 31st spread out. For the first time in the war I actually dropped my bicycle to the ground and readied my rifle to fire.

Slowly, tentatively, with our bodies hunched over, our senses tingling with anticipation, we moved forward.

There was no one in the village. Speck, however, was not convinced that we were safe. His face was etched with worry as he motioned us to move slowly forward. We cleared the village and came upon a large meadow covered with long, brown, gently waving tall grass, bordering a thick pine forest. Speck's eyes were spinning in panic. His orders were terse, "Set up the machine guns. Everyone else spread out and lay low in the tall grass. Sergeant Schwarz, report immediately!"

Speck whispered something to Schwarz. The sergeant retreated quickly back into the village. For several minutes the only sound was the burning buildings. Suddenly, to the far left of us, there was a sharp explosion in the forest. This was followed by two more explosions. Off into the distance we could see the outline of Schwarz heaving hand grenades into the trees.

The explosions opened the gates of hell. Russian soldiers emitting their terrifying war cry came storming out of the forest into the meadow. Speck threw his right arm up and the machine guns of the 31st spewed hundreds of bullets into the attackers. Those of us with rifles lifted ourselves into a kneeling stance and shot at the Russians, trying to outflank our position. The lethal burst was over in a few minutes. There were no Russian survivors.

For several minutes Speck ordered us not to move. The waiting and heavy quiet of the meadow was tense. Finally our kommandant commanded a few men to investigate the forest. Nothing.

The evening was spent burying the dead Russians and looting whatever we deemed worthwhile from them. Horrid work. Over one hundred and fifty Russians had met their end. No one from the 31st was harmed. The result is another good example of how poorly led the Russians are, and conversely how well directed the Germans are. Speck and Lichtwasser are, from a military standpoint, excellent leaders.

Despite the cool of the season we will spend the night sleeping on the meadow's soft tall grass, under a million stars. As the soldiers murmured their good nights I noticed Schwarz standing at a distance, silhouetted by the light of the moon. He was commended by Speck for his courage today. He still scares me though and I hate him for that.

Good night, my sweet angel.

Ludwig

10 December 1914

Dear Elise,

The weather has gotten colder. It rains, snows, and rains, and snows again. The dusty roads of Russia have become bogs, making it impossible to move heavy military equipment. My bicycle and my body are constantly covered in muck as I try to get messages delivered in a timely fashion. Because of these terrible weather conditions we are hunkered down in trenches, not far from where we fired at the Russians in the meadow. The rain, mud, lack of food and sleep all contribute to our pitiful state. We are constantly sick with the flu and a hundred other ailments, plus tension from the constant attacks and bombardment of the Russians makes our life miserable. Mail has been slow to arrive from Germany so encouragement from home has been sparse. When it does arrive I am always thrilled with how happy it makes my comrades. My angel will never send me a letter, but that is all right. Imagining what it would be like is almost as good. Lichtwasser and I are still perplexed with what Schwarz does to his one letter. The fact that he always receives one during each and every mail call is interesting. Someone must truly care for him, yet he always destroys the letter without opening it. Surely it is a key to why he is so gloomy and mean.

Once in a while, usually after the mail is delivered and I am through imagining a letter from you, I plunge, like a rock falling in a deep pond, into loneliness. It feels hollow, like there is nothing inside me. It aches my heart and mind; it is hard to fathom that there is no human on earth who really knows me or cares. I was loved, I have known it. To know love is to have meaning. What else is real? Jesus suffered loneliness, deprivation, betrayal from those who proclaimed their love for Him, and finally a gruesome death. Yet, He rose again and triumphed over death and loneliness. At times I feel God's peace, His purpose for my life. I try to hang on to that, since without it my life is nothing, a vapor, a brief meaningless shadow passing over the land. Oh Lord, You love me! That is a great wonder!

Yet, yet, yet, I wish I had someone. The agony of my skin, the reality of how it makes me subhuman hits me like a bullet in the heart! Sure, most of the 31st respects me, even cares about me, and I don't have to wear glasses and a shawl around them, but to have someone I can call my own, like I wish it was with you, Angel, eludes me. And I think it will elude me for the rest of my life. Agony! Lord, where are You? The bicycle pulls my mind away from darkness. Once I get on the bicycle I pedal so far and so hard that the emotion, the madness of loneliness, collapses in exhaustion and I can cling on to hope again. The hope of a better place with those who love me, those I know would still love me despite the condition of my skin. A place where there is no pain, where life is sweet, forever and ever. God, I long to leave for it now, but I know I must wait till my time. Lord, help me! I am so weak and tired! I am tired of doing good! Lord!

Oh, my angel, Elise! Thank you for your eyes and the hope they bring me!

Ludwig

14 December 1914

Dear Elise,

On a bitterly cold and dark night, I returned with orders that would not be received with great joy. The 31st was ordered to march, immediately, to a point on the front line that was considered weak and thus susceptible to a Russian attack. The march would take at least five hours. Soldiers were roused out of their sleep and the trek began. Speck ordered me to cycle ahead to inform those at our destination to have food and fire ready. I mounted my bicycle and pedaled away. It took me several hours before I finally arrived. My nerves were absolutely shredded from riding so long in the dark. I quickly gave Speck's request to the slumbering kommandant who, unhappy that he had been roused at an ungodly hour by a lowly cyclist, dismissed me with a curt nod. Using the weak beam of my flashlight, I groped around in the dark before I finally found a place near a large tree to bed down. Despite my heavy army coat and extra blanket, the cold seeped into me. There was nothing to do but tear off a few pine boughs and these provided some warmth. Sleep was erratic for me that night.

The sun was creeping over the eastern horizon when the 31st, led by the resolute Speck, Lichtwasser, and Schwarz, finally arrived. Many of the men were so exhausted that they simply threw themselves on the frozen ground and went to sleep right where they landed. A few soldiers had lost their way in the dark or given up. This has happened before during nighttime marches. Most men eventually find their way back in a few days, either alone or in pairs. A few, though, have never returned.

Despite the cold morning hour I did the daily scrub of my clothes. An infestation of lice has joined our company. Only scalding water and powerful bleach provides any resistance to those little beasties. So my two sets of army issue clothing are constantly being cleaned, dried, worn, washed, and cleaned. Over and over again.

Many in the 31st are hoping that the war will be over by Christmas. It is less than two weeks away. I do not think we will be going home soon, but I dream. Going home to my humble abode and then seeing you every Thursday would be a welcome respite from this madness and the haughty glares from Sergeant Schwarz.

Good night, my angel, Elise,

Ludwig

17 December 1914

Dear Elise,

Christmas is getting closer, but the end of the war is definitely not. The rains and intermittent snowfall have stopped. Now it is just cold. The ground is freezing up, which makes digging out trenches difficult. We must first break the ground with a pickaxe to get at the softer dirt underneath. It is hard work. Brutal. The Russians have massed themselves about two hundred meters away in their own well-protected trenches. We bomb each other constantly and take turns attacking each other, but we haven't gained a centimeter of new Russian territory in two weeks. There is speculation that the enemy is bringing thousands of new recruits to the front in a few days. Based on their now stout resistance the Russians also seem to be getting better organized. If this is really true we'll be soon running back to Prussia in a great hurry.

My duties these days are straightforward. Head back to Germany every morning, about a fifty kilometer ride, and report to Kommandant Wolf, who has remained at our last position with the 67th, a company of about two hundred men. We exchange messages and mail bags. Then I turn back to the 31st.

Due to the Christmas season the number of letters and packages that Kommandant Wolf gets forwarded to him for the 31st from Germany is staggering. For all of us, spending the holidays in a trench in Russia is hard to comprehend. Christmas was once a wonderful time of the year for me, but the *fire* destroyed all that. The 24th of December (when Christmas is celebrated in Germany) has been like any other day for me. Lonely. Yet, the loneliness I am feeling is being exacerbated by the presence of Schwarz who has been given a small respite from his duties by Speck and Lichtwasser. As a result he lingers impatiently around the rest of the 31st causing tension just by his presence. The sergeant has not spoken to me for weeks, but during the fleeting moments when our eyes meet waves of dread course through my body. Schwarz's eyes are ice as are mine. Our mutual dislike for one another borders on madness. God, I know, is trying to reach me, to have me love my enemy, but the bitterness I have collected since the fire sits heavy in my spirit. I need to let it go, but I find it too difficult.

Please pray for me, my angel, Elise.

Ludwig

24 December 1914

Dear Elise,

I decided to do something about my loneliness over Christmas. On one of my journeys to the 67th I took a quick side tour and commissioned a Prussian baker to bake several small loaves of white bread a day before the 24th. This cost nearly a month's wages, but it turned out to be a sacrifice worth making.

Just before Christmas Eve dinner, I came up to each man of the 31st and gave them a loaf. It was a great luxury because we had not eaten white bread since leaving for war. Many hugged me in gratitude, shed a tear, and gave me a small token from a package that they had received. When Lichtwasser got his bread, he looked into my eyes for several seconds. Then he pulled out a large piece of chocolate from his pocket and pressed it into my hand. "Merry Christmas," he said quietly.

By the time I had given each man some bread, my sack, which I had used to carry the white bread, was loaded with chocolate, coffee, jam, and cigarettes, even though I steadfastly refuse to smoke them. Still they are excellent for bartering and I have procured plenty of food and candy due to the men's smoking habits.

There was one loaf left when I approached Schwarz. He was standing alone near the nightly bonfire. The light of the fire danced red and yellow on his face. I silently held out the last loaf to him. It was a peace offering. He looked at the bread for a moment and then looked down at me. For a moment his eyes reflected compassion. Stiffly I said, "Sergeant Schwarz, I believe in God and in His Son Jesus Christ. Jesus is the prince of peace and I want to have peace with you. Please take this gift." Schwarz looked at me for a moment, shook his head no, turned, and walked away.

Lichtwasser, who had inadvertently watched the exchange I had with Schwarz, came up to me and said with a smile, "You are a great and courageous man for offering Schwarz a loaf of bread. In many ways you are stronger than Schwarz or any of us. Well, at least you will have a loaf for yourself."

"Yes, sir." I sighed, dejected.

"Come closer to the fire, Schmidt, so you can get some encouragement," said Lichtwasser.

I did, and as the men sang old German Christmas carols I let myself relax. The singing was beautiful and I felt some peace. Much later, as we headed for our posts or beds of straw I passed by Schwarz who was lying on his bedding staring up to the stars. He could not see me in the night's shadows. I stopped and looked at him for the longest time. I prayed for compassion, a godly love for the sergeant. I prayed for my enemy. Yet peace was fleeting; I carry too much hurt, and finally, after several minutes, I quietly walked away.

That night I prayed for you, Elise, and all the men of the 31st who have shown such kindness to me. I also prayed for Sergeant Schwarz.

Merry Christmas, Angel Elise,

Ludwig

Christmas Day 1914

Dear Elise,

December 25, 1914 was one of the most unusual days that I have ever experienced. Usually our mornings start with the thundering of Russian artillery blasting our positions. We always return in kind. Not this day.

Speck ordered us to our posts, but there was no command to fire or attack. I stood with my bicycle ready to relay messages, but there were no messages to relay. So I remained standing quietly like the others. For hours.

Around noon there was a sudden commotion. A soldier named Berger started walking into "No Man's Land" (*the area between the German and Russian trenches*) and headed toward the Russian trenches, armed only with a stout, one meter high Christmas tree and a bottle of wine. The tree was adorned with Wurstals and illuminated by several little flashlights that were hung here and there on the branches. Berger walked calmly, as if he was on a Sunday afternoon stroll. When he was about fifty meters from the Russian position he stopped, put the tree and wine bottle down, and waved a small white handkerchief. Then he turned and walked casually back to our trenches.

We were absolutely shaking with nervous apprehension. Who was going to shoot first? What in the world was Berger thinking? Nothing happened!

Berger got into the safety of our trenches and Speck bellowed at him for not following regulations, for endangering himself and the rest of the company. After the yelling was over Berger returned to his post with a little grin on his face. Our own faces could not help but crease into smiles as well.

For two hours we stared in silence at that odd Christmas tree until finally a slight breeze came up, causing the flashlights to tinkle against each other. The sound seemed to wake up the enemy for suddenly an unarmed Russian soldier emerged from his trench carrying a large brown sack. He was a short, skinny, young man, with thick blond hair trying to escape from the confines of a dirty brown cap. One of my comrades quickly gave him a nickname: Shorty. There was immediate tension from our side and guns were lifted for firing. Speck waved them down. Shorty nervously walked up to the Christmas tree and bent down on one knee. He reached into his sack. The German rifles rose up again, but this time Speck said, "Do not fire until I say so."

Shorty slowly brought out four bottles of vodka, ten tins of caviar, and an envelope. He placed it all underneath the tree. He then put the wine bottle, Wurstals, and flashlights carefully into his sack, leaving the little tree, bare and forlorn. Slowly Shorty stood up, faced our trenches, and bowed deeply. Then he turned around and, unlike Berger, he shuffled quickly back to the safety of his trenches.

There was a long pause. Only the wind rushing through the zone between the opposing trenches could be heard. Speck broke the pause by curtly growling, "Well, Berger, what are you waiting for? Go get that vodka and caviar!"

Berger gulped, saluted, and squeaked, "Can't you order someone else, sir? I already went."

"Not a chance! This was your bird-brained idea from the start, which again, by the way, you did not ask permission for! Now get going!"

"Yes, sir," stuttered Berger.

So off Berger went with a sack of his own and a white hanky that he waved wildly in the direction of the Russians. The silence and tension was, again, thick as bean soup. Berger arrived at the stout, now naked Christmas tree, stooped down and collected the Russian goods and put them in his sack. Like the one before him, he bowed at his benefactors, and then, with a smug smile, sauntered back to us.

There was a little note that the Russians had included in their offerings. It read:

To Our Dear German Comrades,

Thank you for your thoughtful gifts. While most of us do not celebrate Christmas till January 6, we wish you a Merry Christmas! It is so sad that we cannot get to know one another in a more peaceful circumstance. May God have mercy on us all.

Sincerely,

Your Russian Comrades

Christmas 1914 will never be forgotten because for one day sanity reigned in our world. No fighting, a few smiles; even Schwarz seemed disinterested in tormenting me. I felt the odd sensation of peace.

The next morning, however, we were welcomed with the thunder of the Russian artillery. The little naked Christmas tree received a direct hit from a misfired bomb about noon and was obliterated. Later, during an attack by the enemy, I witnessed Sergeant Schwarz kill two Russian soldiers with only a bayonet. Blood from his victims sprayed over the sergeant's face. The surviving attackers soon retreated after that, and Schwarz, with blood still smeared all over him, walked back to the command station. As he entered the ragged building he just happened to pass by me as I was heading out with orders from Speck. Quickly and quietly, so that only I could hear, he said, "Your death will come soon."

The words, the way he said it, and the mad look of his eyes framed in a dirty, unshaven face streaked with blood chilled me to the core.

Pray for me, Elise.

Ludwig

16 January 1915

Dear Elise,

Sorry that I have not written to you in the last few weeks. The war has dulled me into gray. The cold, the death, the destruction, the lack of food and shelter, the mental grind of living on the precipice of life and death takes its toll. Death to at least one member of the 31st seems to occur daily. Death does not discriminate.

It is cold, cold, cold, cold, cold. I am always cold; sleep comes fitfully. I am too cold. The cold freezes my joints; I can barely pedal my bicycle. The ground is frozen and covered by a sheath of snow. The sky is a cold gray. I am cold!

The cold has also frozen our weapons of mayhem and destruction. Messages and mail have slowed down considerably since Christmas so today I received a new duty. My latest job is to obtain horse-drawn wagons from farmers. They are used to cart the wounded or dead from the battleground. Finding the wagons has been relatively easy; what is hard is finding sturdy horses to pull them. Most horses in the war zone have either died of starvation or been slaughtered for food. Yet a few of my comrades found two sturdy mares, wandering aimlessly around a burned out Russian village. Thankfully there are a few farmers here in the 31st. They quickly determined that the two horses were too old and tough for eating and would be much more useful pulling wagons loaded with the dead or wounded. The white horse is now known as Aunt Bertha and the black is Oma (grandma) Rosie. The two new recruits have enjoyed the attention of the 31st. The farmers maintain them with hard-earned water and hay found in ruined and deserted farms. Neck rubs keep the two horses happy as well. If only humans were so easy to maintain.

Kommandant Speck with his usual macabre humor has insisted that if he dies on Russian soil that either Oma Rosie or Aunt Bertha must immediately cart him into Germany. Under no circumstances did he want his body to cool off in enemy territory. Five days after Speck made that terrible declaration he was found dead at his post. The kommandant had been suffering a severe lung infection for a few days. When he started coughing up blood, the end was inevitable. Oma Rosie pulled him to a German military train and it chugged back to Germany before his body had turned cold. We buried him in the graveyard of a small, bombed-out Prussian church. Kommandant Speck's last wish had been fulfilled.

Captain Lichtwasser has been promoted as the new head kommandant of the 31st. We are all grateful. He is a good man. Yet Schwarz, now unfettered by Speck, will probably be more relentless in expressing his intense hatred toward me.

Sweet Angel, I have had enough of this war. Pray for me.

Ludwig

24 January 1915

Dear Elise,

With heavy artillery non-functional due to the cold and soldiers barely keeping themselves warm it had been relatively quiet on the Eastern Front for several days. Little did we know that this tense quiet would embolden packs of starving wolves to desperate measures. It was at dusk five days ago, just as the sun was setting behind a bitterly cold, gray and white sky, that the uneasy stillness was shattered by the howling of wolves, seemingly dozens of them. They came out of the forest like a sudden storm and attacked us and our enemy. The anguished screams of young Hans Weber, who was viciously overwhelmed by a pack sent us scurrying for our rifles. We fired at the wolves in a desperate attempt to save Weber and to survive ourselves. It was soon over as the bullets found their marks and eliminated several of the savage predators. Shaken to the core we staggered over to Weber who was bleeding from his throat and legs. We hurriedly transported him to the medic who saved his life, but the war was over for Weber due to his injuries.

The next few days were madness. Packs of wolves, crazed and fearless due to starvation, attacked both us and the Russians. They would come running at us relentlessly, wave after wave, howling, snarling, growling, ruthless eyes shimmering, hellish in the weak winter light. The war with the Russians ceased as we both fought for our very survival from the wolves' nightmarish pursuit of us. Despite killing off dozens, new packs of wolves quickly replaced the slain.

During a break from the attacks, Shorty, the same Russian who at Christmas time brought us vodka and caviar to the Christmas tree, approached us, armed only with a white flag. Speck commanded a rather reluctant Berger to shuffle off with a white flag as well and find out what our short Russian delicacy provider wanted. Berger and Shorty stood in no mans' land for the longest time. Occasionally an odd chuckle could be heard. After fifteen minutes or so Speck bellowed for Berger to wrap it up, while a gruff Russian command was also heard. Berger and Shorty laughed one more time together, shook hands, and ambled back to their trenches. What happened next was remarkable.

Speck got a message from the Russian commander that they wanted to suspend hostilities to figure out how to eliminate the wolf problem. Speck agreed. For the next three days, we collaborated with the Russians to kill off the scourge that wanted to decimate us. We baited the wolves with poisoned meat, we emptied our machine guns at the packs, we lit fires, and finally after three days, the wolf problem had been solved—at least on our part of the front. Reluctantly we then resumed the grisly business of trying to kill the Russians who helped save our lives from wolves. Madness.

Good night, Elise.

Ludwig

30 January 1915

Dear Elise,

Today, on a bitterly cold, overcast day, just as the sun had grudgingly made its upward ascent turning the landscape from black to gray, we endured a sudden surge from the Russians. They outnumbered us by a wide margin. They pushed us back out of our trenches. Hard. I only had time to release the rifle from my precious bicycle and run with the others. Trying to cycle on the road now overrun by Russian soldiers or trying to ride on rough terrain would have been foolish.

As we scrambled away to save our precious lives I became detached from the main body of the 31$_{st}$ and ended up with a small group of about twenty men. A hail storm of bullets flew all around us in our desperate retreat. There were so many bullets that the soldiers who got hit by them thudded instantly to the frozen, snow-covered surface, without a cry. Death came that fast. Those of us who had somehow survived this barrage managed to run into a small grove of trees, which gave us some respite. When the Russians lost sight of us, they stopped shooting.

The grove gave way to an endless, empty bog. Running into it would leave us completely exposed and vulnerable to the enemy. Running into the bog meant death. So we hunkered down, coaxing our frozen rifles to life by blowing on the trigger or bullet chamber, desperately trying to get them to work. We could see the Russians bobbing slowly through the trees toward us. They were no more than thirty meters away. There were also about twenty-five Russians, fifty to seventy meters away on our left and right flanks. We were being encircled, trapped in a kettle of rifles, bayonets, and an imminent brutal death.

Suddenly! Boom, boom, phffft, boom, the grove rocked with artillery fire. German artillery fire! The Russians stopped their bobbing for a moment. Phffft boom! Three of them suddenly went airborne, twisting, flipping like rag dolls thrown up into the sky. A German cry went up, causing the rattle of several machine guns to go off at once. It kept those of us in the grove sprawled to the ground. Thousands of bullets whistled above our heads. Standing up would be suicide. Since my mind was drowning in terror from the tumult around me, I at first did not comprehend the heavy weight that suddenly thudded onto my back and the blunt, cold, metal that was pushed into my neck. The weight pressed harder, causing me to gasp. Twisting my head sideways to look up, my heart nearly came to an abrupt stop. It was Schwarz lying on top of me with a pistol trembling in his dirty, gnarled right hand. The barrel of the gun shook painfully against my Adam's apple.

Schwarz in panic screamed, "Protect me, Schmidt! As your superior officer I order you to stand and shoot back!"

Countless bullets were still flying through the grove. My legs froze as my brain tried to make sense of the predicament I was in. Schwarz yelled above the chaos and carnage all around us. "Stand up! Fight! That is an order!"

I refused to obey. The crossfire in the grove would kill me in an instant if I stood up.

Schwarz screamed into my face. "Stand up or I am going to shoot your ugly head off!"

"No!" I screamed back. "I don't want to die! Never!"

Schwarz's hand trembled violently as he kept the pistol pressed against my neck. Suddenly a bomb screeched through the air, just above our heads. It split the earth with a resounding crash no more than ten meters from us. The impact from the blast was so severe that the sergeant got knocked over a few meters away from me. For several moments I continued to lie on my chest, temporarily stunned, my ears ringing from the blast. Then I became aware of someone screaming nearby. Slowly I rolled onto my back. Through the haze of my shell-shocked mind and the dust that had been kicked up I saw Schwarz, only two meters away from me, frantically moving around on all fours. He muttered to himself. "My gun! Where is my gun?"

The sergeant then glared at me and screamed, "Once I find my gun I'm going to shoot you for insubordination and treason! I'm going to execute you and no one will know!"

My rifle was lying at my side. Gingerly I reached for it and blew off dirt from the trigger. I readied it to fire and then rolled onto my front and waited. The sergeant finally found his gun and triumphantly picked it up. He screamed, "I am going to execute you now Schmidt!" The gun was clogged with dirt. It was as he frantically brushed and blew it off that he suddenly saw the barrel of my rifle pointed at his head. He froze. There was a long pause, the mayhem of the battle faded as our eyes locked together for the last time. There was fear and disbelief in Schwarz's eyes. Mine were ice. A thousand thoughts swept through my mind in the few seconds we looked into each other's eyes. One stood out. I could not keep my promise to God and treasure Schwarz's life anymore. It was mine or his. I made a decision. Even though I was an average marksman, the shot was straightforward. I pulled the trigger. The bullet entered Schwarz's forehead in an instant and he was dead before his face crashed to the earth.

The ground vibrated from another bomb blast, causing my mind to flicker a moment into darkness, then light, then back to dark.

Lichtwasser found me unconscious by the dead Sergeant Schwarz. Smelling salts revived me. The captain guided me to Aunt Bertha and her cart. As the horse trudged forward I viewed the destruction of battle. Dead Russians and Germans, destroyed military hardware, trees splintered by bombs, all jumbled about in a wild mess. Terrible.

Aunt Bertha brought me to a makeshift infirmary near our regained position. The battle had not solved anything. The Germans and Russians were back exactly where they had been before the surge. A doctor diagnosed me. Severe shell shock. A few days of bed rest was prescribed.

Lichtwasser visited me later in the evening. He informed me that my saviors from the grove had been a small detachment from the 89th Company. Fortunately they were well equipped with ammunition, artillery, and machine guns that were all in working order. They had eliminated over eighty Russians and captured fifty. As for the twenty members of the 31st who had gone into the grove only seven had come out. Lichtwasser was not happy that we had become separated from the rest of the company, but with my ears still ringing from the bombs and traumatized by what I had seen and done, that was irrelevant. I would serve in the Kaiser's army again. My fine bicycle had, like myself, miraculously survived and been retrieved.

After Lichtwasser had finished briefing me he entered into deeper waters. "I found you near Sergeant Schwarz. What can you tell me about his death?"

"Sergeant Schwarz died heroically fighting the enemy," I answered in a montone.

"Did you fight alongside him?"

"Yes."

Lichtwasser sighed and looked deep into my eyes. "Is that all?" I stared back. "Yes."

"Are you sure?"

It took much too long for me to say, "Yes."

I knew Lichtwasser believed I was lying and I was overcome with deep remorse. The captain was my advocate. His respect for me, his dignified treatment, his declaration of friendship to me had given me hope. It had given me life. To lie to this man was devastating. However, I remained silent.

Lichtwasser stared at me for a long time before uttering quietly, "Very well. I will report to Schwarz's mother and my superiors that the sergeant died a hero. I will now let you rest. That is all."

He left after we had stiffly saluted one another.

I did not sleep a minute that night. The reality of ruthlessly killing Schwarz and lying about it to an advocate and friend was too much for me. God, what have I done?

The next morning, just as the sun started to lift above the eastern horizon, I left the infirmary, despite doctor's orders, and found Lichtwasser sitting alone at a table near a shed that had served as his lodgings for the night. He was sipping a coffee staring ahead in deep reflection. A lone candle flickered grudgingly providing a touch of light. It was cold and outside of the minute candle light despairingly gray. Lichtwasser looked at me warily when I announced my presence.

"Yes, Schmidt, what can I do for you?" he said evenly.

Overcome with remorse I sputtered, "I lied to you yesterday."

Lichtwasser dryly said, "I know. I have dealt with hundreds of men and have gained an acute sense of who is telling the truth or not. Quite frankly, Schmidt, you have no skill in lying as you are a man of integrity. Now before you say anything more I am going to remind you that as your commanding officer I hold the power to have you court martialed and executed for insubordination or murder. Will you be putting me in that position where I must order your execution? Have you thought this out clearly, Schmidt?

"Your respect and dignity for me over the last several months has given me hope and life. I believe it has been a gift from God. It is difficult for me to betray what you have given me, but I did yesterday. I want to make amends."

Lichtwasser smiled. "You have earned my respect and trust with your excellent work as a cyclist, but more importantly with your character. You are my friend and a highly valued member of the 31st, Schmidt."

"I want to tell you the truth about Sergeant Schwarz."

"No. Like you said, Sergeant Schwarz died honorably defending Germany and the Kaiser."

"But..."

"No! You will not talk about what really happened in that grove. There has been far too much death in this war already. The 31st needs you. I believe you are a good man. My superiors, however, do not care if you are a good man. I believe if you tell them the truth you will likely die. I don't want that. Please don't breathe a word."

Lichtwasser pulled out a letter from his coat pocket. "About a month ago I found a torn up envelope near my post. Despite the condition of it, I was still able to discern that it was sent to Schwarz. I was also able to make out the return address and so I sent a letter to it. I introduced myself and explained the situation of Schwarz with the 31st and yourself.

"Two days ago I received a very interesting reply to this letter from Schwarz's *mother*. She wrote that fifteen years ago Sergeant Schwarz witnessed the death of his father in a sword duel. The dispute was over some ridiculously trivial matter concerning a level of treatment that the elder Schwarz had expected from a certain individual. This was not the first time that Herr Schwarz had risked his life and reputation over some matter concerning his honor. He was an officer in the Prussian army, and although his service was exemplary, his vanity was not.

"Herr Schwarz's last duel was against a man who from a physical and social aspect was considered far inferior to the Prussian officer. Officer Schwarz was so confident that he would quickly dispatch this "lower man" that, unbeknownst to his wife, he brought his young son, the future Sergeant Schwarz, to witness the duel.

"The sword fight, despite a dire warning from the smaller man that he would kill Officer Schwarz, went on as planned. It was over in seconds. The shorter man was brilliant with the sword and extinguished Officer Schwarz, in front of his son, with a lethal thrust of his weapon into Schwarz's abdomen.

"The demise of his father and the lack of honor it brought affected Schwarz profoundly. As he grew up his anger and disdain for those he considered inferior got him constantly reprimanded at school. It only got worse when his mother remarried a man he considered unworthy. The tension between the young Schwarz and his new stepfather became so great that the future sergeant was eventually enrolled into a military boarding school. During this time Schwarz constantly suffered negative consequences from his superiors for bullying. Yet Schwarz's brilliance in military tactical maneuvering and ruthless efficiency as a soldier overshadowed his faults.

"It is obvious that Sergeant Schwarz never recovered from witnessing the untimely and dishonorable death of his father. It severely traumatized him. He became a man incapable of being loved or one to extend love. Only his mother, who week after week sent a letter to him but never received any reply, loved him. Now her son is dead, but can you imagine the added grief she would experience if I wrote to her saying that he died dishonorably on the battlefield and he tore up every letter he received from her without reading a single word?

"No. Unlike his father's death, Sergeant Schwarz has died honorably in battle. That is what I will be writing to his mother, Schmidt. That is what I will include in the report to my superiors. And as for you, Schmidt, you are never to bring this matter up again. Is that clear?"

"Yes sir."

Good night, Angel.

Ludwig

5 February 1915

Dear Elise,

You shall not murder. (Exodus 20:13)

Schwarz is dead. My actions killed him. It is very clear in the Bible. "You shall not murder." It is still hard for me to grasp what I have done. It was God who prevented me from murdering Sergeant Schwarz in the trench several months ago. I am thankful for that. My rage toward Schwarz and the intent to murder him at that time was a sin. My evil thoughts toward him were a sin. I battled hard with God against those thoughts. However, in the grove there was a clear intention that Schwarz wanted to kill me. I could have wounded him, but would his evil torment of me have ended? I don't believe so. The reality was that I had an opportunity to live. The alternative was to wait and eventually be brutally executed by a man who promised he would. God have mercy on me. I did not want to die; I did not want to follow the mad orders of someone with a low disregard for my life. I would have died had I done so. All I wanted was to live. Forgive me, Father, for killing what you have created, but you must understand! Angel, please forgive me!

Lichtwasser had Schwarz's corpse brought to the same graveyard where Speck lies. He was honored as a hero of the German Reich. No one wept at the burial. Now, several days later after the incident in the grove, no one mentions Schwarz's name. It was as if he had never existed. The relief to be free from his inhumanity gives us all life, particularly myself. What a horrible thing to write. God have mercy on me, but that is what I truly feel. Lichtwasser checks up on me constantly asking how I am and encouraging me with kind words. It is helping a lot.

We marched deeper into Russia today. Lichtwasser had me relaying messages between the other advancing companies of the German army. By noon my legs were burning from pedaling my bicycle over the snow-covered trails that the Russians call roads.

A scouting patrol brought back important news to us later in the afternoon. The Russians may have finally found someone to organize them. Thousands of Russian soldiers are massing together. They are only five kilometers from our position, are well equipped, and are maneuvering in concise patterns. Lichtwasser and the other kommandants have made a hard decision. The enemy may lose a far greater number of soldiers than us in one or two battles, but because of their numerical advantage and apparent organization they will eventually overrun us.

The order to fall back was greeted with derision from some members of the 31st. Not another march! Why did we come all this way into Russia? On the other hand the prospect of leaving this backward, depressing country would be wonderful.

Tonight the sky was lit up with Russian and German bombs trying to outdo one another. The bombs' explosions were spectacular and set against the night sky were a wonder to behold.

At 5:30 in the morning, a few hours after the bombing had ended from both sides, Lichtwasser gave us the order to march west. Back to Prussia and our old trenches.

Why did we come here in the first place? Until then, sleep well, Angel.

Ludwig

11 February 1915

Dear Elise,

It would have been so easy to travel back to Germany by train, but the Russians have destroyed large sections of the track so that is impossible. As a result we have spent the last several days marching west from sunup to sundown. We are close to our destination, but now Lichtwasser has ordered us to march through the night. Marching during the nighttime hours is never easy simply because we are tired and it is too dark! Logical! However, logic is not an issue with Lichtwasser. His orders are often based on intuition or "an answer to prayer," as he so often puts it. Yet no matter how stupid Lichtwasser's commands seem to be, we have learned to trust them, because in hindsight they always turn out good for the 31st. So far. Still, this march does not make sense. It is so dark that we have to hold on to the shoulder of the man in front of us. Pushing a bike with one hand and holding the shoulder of a man in front of me with the other for several hours was extremely difficult.

The sun finally, grudgingly, rose in the east, and our movements became easier and faster. We hadn't marched long in the light when all of a sudden a lone Russian plane buzzed over us. We took several shots at it to no avail. The plane swooped around us like a vulture, just out of reach, seemingly taunting us. Lichtwasser knew what the plane was doing. It was a reconnaissance aircraft and it provided the Russian land troops a visual of our position. We were underneath the plane. Easy. Thankfully Lichtwasser had made us march through the night so we were well ahead of the Russian ground troops. Despite the stifling fatigue gained from this walk of agony, the 31st suddenly marched with greater urgency to the west. Knowing that hordes of Russians were aware of our position was tremendous motivation to move briskly.

Lichtwasser had me race ahead on my bicycle to Prussia to tell Kommandant Wolf and his 67th Company, the group that had returned to our former border trenches, to be ready for a massive Russian assault.

It took me three hours to pedal back to the old position in Prussia. Kommandant Wolf received my message with grave concern. His soldiers, however, oblivious to the oncoming threat, were the polar opposite of their kommandant. Relaxed and well fed, they had spruced up the trenches by building sturdy wooden barracks and erecting signs with names of streets from their hometowns. It was rather quaint in an odd way. Wolf's order for the men to get to battle stations was received with some incredulity. Having had no combat action for a week had made the soldiers of the 67th rather lethargic. Kommandant Wolf noticed this immediately and he had to growl at them to move quicker. Once the men were in battle stations there was a great lull. Where were the Russians? More critical: where were the retreating Germans?

Several very quiet hours passed by. Just as the men started to give way to sleep from the boredom of waiting, a distinct buzzing sound could be heard. It was a Russian plane. It looked a little different from the one that had been harassing the 31st initially, but it was making the same vulture-like movements as the one I had seen earlier in the morning.

With a shaky voice I explained to Kommandant Wolf what Lichtwasser had said about the Russian aircraft. The 31st and the Russians must be near. Another buzzing sound reached our ears. A German war plane came into view, its machine guns rapidly emptying bullets at the enemy aircraft. The Russian plane banked upward in a desperate attempt to escape the German. Against a terrific blue backdrop, the two aircraft zigged and zagged over top of us, trying to outflank each other. The sounds of the planes' engines, the wind slicing against their wings, and the occasional rattle of the machine guns added terror to the spectacle.

Finally, after about twenty minutes, the German plane managed to get the advantage. A burst came from its machine gun and shortly thereafter, smoke could be seen streaming from the Russian aircraft. Its nose dipped downward and a sharp whining noise, as if the plane was screaming before its imminent death, cut through the air. We were all transfixed at the sight, and when the Russian plane crashed with a mighty explosion in the eastern forest about a kilometer from us, we all cheered in delight. The German plane tilted its wings in a brief salute before heading west. The celebration did not last long.

Kommandant Lichtwasser and the rest of the 31st came into view. They were all running. Lichtwasser was yelling, but at first we could not make it out. Then: "The Russians are coming, the Russians are coming!"

The 67th braced itself for battle. The 31st clambered into the trenches exhausted. Lichtwasser gulped out, "The enemy is no more than thirty minutes behind us. We tried to get away from the Russian airplane by marching through a forest, but we got lost and gave away a lot of time and space to the ground troops. There must be hundreds of them. Are you ready, Kommandant Wolf?"

Wolf smiled thinly, "Oh, we are going to be ready all right." He turned to his lieutenant and ordered, "Gruber, issue these men from the 31st surgical masks immediately! The rest of you get yours ready!

There was a frantic scramble as Gruber and several other soldiers brought us simple surgical masks, covered in gauze, from several sturdy wooden boxes lying nearby. Within minutes every German soldier was wearing a surgical mask, the same that a doctor conducting an operation would wear. *(These crude gas masks would later be replaced by elaborate airtight masks that covered the whole head. Large glass eye holes and a tube attached to an air canister strapped to the back provided sight and a way to breathe.)*

It was cumbersome to man our battle stations with the surgical masks on, but Wolf's orders were not to be questioned. A queasy tension came over all of us as we waited in silence. A hundred butterflies danced in my stomach.

The Russian battle cry, like the first faint rumble of a thunderstorm was heard first. The rumble grew louder and louder until finally we could see them. Russians. Hundreds of them. We were outnumbered at least five to one. The Russians ran as one massive entity at our trenches. Lichtwasser and Wolf screamed their commands over the thunder of the attack.

We fired everything that we had at the enemy from the East. Submachine guns, bombs, rifles, all lit up at once. Many of the Russians fell, but the horde was too large. They kept coming. The noise was deafening. Still, Wolf was able to be heard. "Ceasefire! Make sure your gas masks are on! Ready! Fire the gas!"

Canisters loaded with deadly mustard gas were heaved toward the fierce incoming enemy. They broke apart and the Russians were enveloped in a deadly yellowish cloud. The gas worked quickly with deadly results. It tore up the Russian's lungs, causing them to bleed. They were literally drowning in their own blood. Weakened by the gas, the Russians were no match for the Germans. They were either shot down, bayoneted to death, or succumbed to the mustard gas. Still the enemy came. Wave after wave. Madness.

My job was to provide those manning the submachine guns with a steady supply of ammunition. They rattled out thousands and thousands of bullets. The chaos going on in front of me was straight from the bowels of hell. Finally, a piercing sound of a whistle could be heard above the din. The Russians retreated.

The cloud of gas over the battlefield slowly lifted upward revealing a scene of horror. Countless Russians and a few Germans were strewn in front of the trenches. Most were dead while others groaned their final sounds on earth.

Several hours later, with the surviving Russians back to the same positions that they had inexplicably left several weeks earlier, we set upon the terrible task of looting and burying the dead. The Russians also got out of their trenches and retrieved those that had fallen nearby. It was so strange to see opposing forces, so relatively near to one another, not attacking or shooting each other. Instead the focus was on clearing away the dead from No Man's Land. There were so many that Lichtwasser ordered us to make a mass grave. It took an excruciatingly long time, but once the bodies had been collected we torched them. The smoke and smell from the corpses hung thick in the air. Many men gagged out whatever was in their stomachs.

Something broke in our spirits that day. We had witnessed too much death and destruction. For what? For the Kaiser and Germany? Not good enough. For our own survival? Yes. But how long could we survive against the Russians? Madness. It is all madness!

It was well past midnight when Lichtwasser gave the order for us to retire. There was no campfire, no talking, nothing. We were exhausted and still in shock. After crawling into my nest for the night I wrote to you, Angel.

Then I wept.

Ludwig

18 February 1915

Dear Elise,

The Day that changed everything came in with a spectacular red sunrise, which I admired for several moments. *The Day* also came in with the usual volley of gunfire and bombings from the Russians.

At 10:25 a.m. I was summoned by Kommandant Lichtwasser to bring a message to the 82nd.

"You should be back within two hours," he said.

"Yes, sir," I responded.

Off I went pedaling hard on my bicycle, now rigged with a small two-wheeled cart attached to the back. It had been invaluable in carrying foodstuffs and large mailbags. The 82nd might have some mail for us.

For the first time in ages the sun was actually providing more than just light to the day. The warmth of its beams on my face was a welcome respite from the usual frigid temperatures over the last few months. The warmth also caused the snow and ice covering the innumerable bogs, sloughs, and ponds of the area to start evaporating. Soon I was riding in a fog so thick that I could barely see my hands on the handle bars. This caused me to slow down to a turtle's pace and I braced myself for a sudden meeting of tree or rock.

The fog and silence were unnerving as I crept along. Then, suddenly—phffft, boom, phffft, boom—the disquieting peace was shattered by the whistle of missiles slicing through the air before bursting violently on the ground. I immediately stopped pedaling and sought shelter by curling myself under the metal frame of the cart.

Phffft, boom, phffft, boom, phffft, boom went on incessantly. I heard trees and dirt being burst apart and then felt fine dust drift gently onto my face. An explosion ripped up the trail near where I lay. A sharp pain suddenly scorched up from my right ankle. Another nearby explosion dazed me and the pain subsided.

For several minutes I lay huddled under the cart before I realized there was a sharp tingling feeling coming from my right foot. Looking down I could see that a piece of shrapnel had gone clean through my right boot and had embedded itself into the ankle bone. Blood oozed freely out of the wound. With great caution I delicately touched the affected area with my right hand. Grasping the piece of metal with my thumb and first two fingers I gave a firm pull. The shrapnel didn't budge. Pain enveloped me like a blanket of cut glass. Releasing the shrapnel, I brought the hand up to my face. It was covered in blood. Suppressing a scream trying to blow out from the depths of my stomach, I rolled over onto my back.

Beads of sweat popped out on my forehead. The pain from my ankle rolled on and on like water lapping up onto a beach. Frantically, I grabbed some snow nearby and rubbed it gently on the wound. It dulled the agony somewhat. Panting deeply, I reached for some more snow and carefully placed it on the wound. Suddenly, like the startling crash of lightning on a rainy day, I heard noises.

A grunt, boots scuffling along the gravel, the distinct Russian language sliced through the fog. Terror replaced pain. Another voice, a German voice, could be heard. "Hummel, Hummel." The Russian voices ceased immediately.

"Hummel, Hummel."

Silence.

"Hum..."

The silence erupted into a crescendo of rifle fire, screaming, loud commands, and movement of bodies through brush. How long did I lie underneath the cart while this blind battle raged on? Five minutes, fifteen, half an hour, an hour? I will never know. And as abruptly as it had started, it ended. There was a long silence after the last gunshot echoed through the forest. Sunlight flickered through the fog, awakening me from the paralyzing shock that had come over me. The beams of light evaporated the fog and it lifted gently upward, like a curtain in front of a stage.

Pine and birch trees, the gravel trail, and a scene of destruction came into view. Gingerly and with great difficulty, I lifted myself up to my feet. The ankle throbbed an agonizing protest to my brain, but at least the bicycle and cart were still in one piece. A long sturdy stick that was lying nearby became my crutch, and I used it to hobble around, slowly exploring my now revealed surroundings. Dead Russian and German men lay helter-skelter on the gentle green moss of the forest. Having seen this scene once too often, I blocked it out with the ruthless mental strength I had developed since the war started.

When I first heard the clicking sound of a rifle being cocked my initial reaction was disbelief. What? A gruff Russian voice spoke to my back. The crutch slipped out of my hand and landed on the gravel trail with a clanging sound. The sudden explosion of a gunshot and a bullet whizzing over my head was so terrifying that I crumpled to my knees. The same Russian voice, only louder, assaulted my ears. Raising my arms up I started to whimper the Lord's Prayer under my breath.

Clutching a rifle with shaking hands a Russian soldier walked tentatively into my view. His long, black, scraggly beard waved serenely in the tiny gentle breezes that fluttered through the trees. He was like Blackbeard the pirate, the one I had read so much about, only much skinnier. His gently shifting beard contrasted sharply with his intense bloodshot eyes that glared at me with the fierceness of a wild dog. One of his trembling hands, pale and bony with exceedingly dirty fingernails reached toward the shawl covering my face. It grabbed the cloth, like eagle talons would a fish, and yanked it off, exposing my head in all its mutilated glory.

Blackbeard gasped in shock for a moment and then, with eyes bulging in terror and his mouth mumbling something incoherent, managed to shakily lift the rifle to his shoulder, point its barrel directly at my forehead and press the trigger. Click. Again. Click. Click, click, click. Nothing. Frothing at the mouth in frustration the Russian lifted his rifle to strike me, but then—a miracle. He fainted. Blackbeard just collapsed straight back onto the moss.

Breathing slowly and deeply so as to get my heart beating at a regular rhythm again, I crawled over to Blackbeard and felt his neck for a pulse. Yes, there it was. Beating oddly, but still beating. There was a stain on the right shoulder of his great coat. Upon further inspection I found a bullet hole in the middle of the stain. Pulling the coat partway down his right shoulder revealed a bloody flesh wound that if not treated soon would lead to infection. Obviously Blackbeard was suffering from some blood loss as well. It was imperative that I get him some medical attention. *Yet this man had tried to kill me. Why help someone so intent on my destruction? I could easily kill him or just bike away and let him bleed to death. This is war!* These thoughts and many others screamed in my mind. Then God's voice spoke quietly to my heart and I knew what to do. Grace.

My near-death experience had filled my body with a rush of adrenaline and it dulled the pain of my wound. It also gave me the energy to drag Blackbeard to the cart by his legs. With every particle of strength left in me I heaved the Russian onto my shoulder and plopped him hard into the cart. Thankfully Blackbeard was short and very skinny. No doubt he had been on a diet similar to the German soldiers, and he fit, albeit awkwardly, in the cart. Still, the exertion winded me and it took several moments for me to regain my breath.

Time in the forest had flitted away to late afternoon. The gentle warm breezes that had been flowing through the trees turned cool and the tree shadows lengthened. Pulling off a great coat from a slain Russian, I threw it on Blackbeard. Suddenly, I had an idea. It took several minutes, but I removed the clothing from Blackbeard and replaced them with the uniform of a dead German. No doubt a German doctor would have more inclination to treat a fellow comrade than one from the enemy. Before getting onto the bicycle I found some more snow and put it down my right boot. Soon, the wounded ankle was numb again and I headed back from where I had come, hoping desperately that this ordeal would soon be over.

Although my new Russian companion was short and lean, he was still a load, and sweat poured off of me as I pedaled the bicycle forward. The landscape, now freed from its foggy veil, was beautiful. Pine and birch trees, interspersed with meadows and icy ponds, went by me and the unconscious Russian lying in the cart. Every so often I stopped to stuff more snow down my right boot. Progress was steady, despite the pain in my ankle.

Finally, as the sun made its last flicker of the day, I heard the German language. It wasn't my company that I met that evening. They were remnants of the 52nd. The pain from the ankle wound had become so great by then that the transfer of myself and Blackbeard by the 52nd to a nearby medical unit became disjointed due to my slipping in and out of consciousness.

I woke up in a crowded makeshift hospital located in a bombed-out church. There seemed to be hundreds of patients, all lying on simple cots side by side. I peered over to the bed next to me. Piercing eyes, a small smile, and a scraggly black beard stared back at me. Blackbeard! He reached out his hand and I reached out to hold it. We held our hands as brothers would for a long time.

A doctor came by and asked about myself and Blackbeard. I lied, telling him that we both were part of the 31st company and had just survived an intense battle. Blackbeard must have suffered a severe concussion because he now had trouble speaking and hearing. The doctor nodded with a somewhat skeptical face, but informed me that Blackbeard's injury had already been operated on and that his full recovery was certain.

As for myself, I was slated for an operation later that day. A sudden cry from a neighboring patient caught the doctor's attention and he drifted away. I'll write more after the operation.

Until then, Angel,

Ludwig

22 February 1915

Dear Elise,

Due to the unhygienic conditions of this makeshift hospital, many of the wounded soldiers are losing limbs or dying due to infection. I fear I am included in this horror. The shrapnel was removed from my right ankle. However, it was not soon enough to prevent my foot from becoming severely infected and for gangrene to set in. As a result of this reality the doctor was forced to saw off my entire right foot to prevent the spread of infection from the wound. Unfortunately the amputation was also too late. Infection caused by the shrapnel has assaulted my blood and every vital organ. The nurses and doctors say with their mouths that there is a chance that I will recover, but their eyes say no. If God allows my survival, what will He have in store for me? A career as a cyclist will prove to be difficult with only one foot.

There is a severe lack of medicine, so painkillers are reserved for those in far greater need. It is hard to believe that my pain does not warrant more. The agony from the infection is excruciating and wreaks havoc with my body and mind. Only when my arm muscles start to twitch involuntarily and my mouth makes gurgling noises and emits frothy spit does a doctor give me a dose of painkiller.

The last injection was just ten minutes ago so I have a few moments of sanity and control to write you this bittersweet letter, which may be my last. Three days have passed since Blackbeard and I were brought to this hospital. My Russian friend continues to lie next to my bed, but seems to be recovering nicely. At times he nods and smiles at me. When I writhe in pain he holds my hand and yells something incomprehensible until some nurse or doctor arrives. No one seems to have any suspicion that he is Russian.

All the soldiers in this place are in various stages of duress; their screams of anguish never stop. Bloody bodies, some alive, some dead, stream back and forth out of this broken down church all day and night. The seven doctors and twenty-odd nurses are exhausted because all they do is saw, slice, cut, sew, and inject serum into ruined bodies. Constantly. Their hands and arms are always red with the blood of the wounded and dead.

Sleep, if and when it comes over me, is a whirlwind of emotion. Nightmares of battles that never end eventually wake me up, gasping and crying. Yet lately, the nightmares have been broken with a dream that can only be described as *bliss*.

It starts with me gently drifting like a small patch of fog high on a wispy air current. Looking down I see a large, perfectly square, perfectly kept, deep green lawn. On each side of this lawn is a riot of flowers of every type and hue. In the middle of the square is my father, dressed in a formal white suit, sitting on a stately chair by a small round golden table. White tea cups and a large golden teapot rest on the table. Nearby, also sitting on white chairs similar to my father's, are my mother and sister. They are both dressed in beautiful white gowns topped with wide-brimmed summer hats. Occasionally they reach for a cup and sip delicately from it. They seem to be enjoying themselves, talking, smiling, with an occasional chuckle. There is a peace at that table that brings rest to my heart. As I drift by I sense this contentment, this quiet euphoria of joy. Yet try as I might I never can land on that lawn. I always just float by. Heaven? It must be a bit of heaven. That is all I can ever remember from this blissful dream. Where do I start from? Where do I end up? I don't know.

The dream ends and then the cries of agony from the wrecked men around me startle my sleep away. Pain crawls onto and into my body and starts cutting every fiber with a razor. The cutting is relentless until, after about an hour, my body is convulsing out of control. Only then does a doctor inject relief into my veins.

Lately, I have tried to fight off the pain by dwelling on you, Elise. What would my life be with you? Together we would slowly meander through wildflower meadows or cool, pine tree forests or narrow, cafe-lined streets with the thick smell of coffee hanging in the air. Long conversations, smiles, holding hands, a sweet kiss. Elise, I became a man over the last few months. If I survive this ordeal, my first stop will be at the Maier's Chocolate Shop. I will look into your eyes. I believe you are like an angel. An angel looks into a man's eyes to know who they are. And you would find me good.

Good-bye, Elise. My angel.

Ludwig

Epilogue: 25 April, 1922

From the files of Albrecht Schneider

Dear Herr Schneider,

My name is Elise von Hitzlenberger. I am the widow of a former business associate of yours, Herr Otto von Hitzlenberger. Although we have never met I trust my late husband's evaluation of your character, namely one of integrity and Christian dignity. I also am aware that you have connections with a few reputable publishing houses. With that in mind, Herr Schneider, I have taken these bold but tentative steps to approach you.

Now I know as a business man you like to get to the heart of the matter in a timely fashion, yet I insist the following lengthy preamble is necessary for you to fully understand the business opportunity I bring before you.

My beloved Otto succumbed to influenza three years ago. I loved him dearly, and after his death I drifted into a very disconcerting melancholy. Even the most mundane activities—getting up in the morning, eating, walking—became complex ordeals that often left me weeping. I was emotionally shattered. Those dreadful, dark days may never have ended until God, and I believe it was His providence, did something extraordinary.

One spring morning, just four months after Otto's death, He brought two gentlemen, one Russian, the other French, to my estate desiring a short audience with me. They had a reference from my old employer, Herr Winifeld Maier, proprietor of the Maier's Chocolate Shop. Due to my mental fragility I was initially quite distressed by this unannounced intrusion into my home. I was also offended at Herr Maier, believing him to be overly presumptuous for directing these foreign intruders to me.

Yet, the gentlemen's dress, manners, Herr Maier's reference, and the Russian's expensive and well-crafted attaché case suggested great wealth or even nobility. I became very intrigued and gave in to my curiosity. Feigning some reluctance, though, I finally ushered them in. I had my housekeeper, Louise, prepare us tea as we sat down in the drawing room.

The Frenchman, an older, stout man, introduced himself as Monsieur Luc Suave, valet and interpreter of the Russian gentleman, Boris Metlevev. He also brushed his lips on each of my cheeks as a way of greeting. I am ashamed to say that this French tradition has always made me blush. Herr Metlevev was a small, slender man with sharp eyes and a well- trimmed black beard. He, unlike the Frenchman, removed his gloves, bowed, gently took my right hand in his, and then carefully touched his lips near my knuckles. This type of greeting was much more acceptable to me.

As Herr Metlevev spoke Russian, Monsieur Suave interpreted. His German was good with just a minor hint of a dignified French accent. After pleading for a pardon due to their abrupt visit and offering condolences for the loss of my beloved Otto, Monsieur Suave provided a quick biography of his master.

Herr Metlevev was the son of a Russian businessman. After the Russian Revolution of 1917, his family fled Russia to France for the freedom to express themselves and the pursuit of financial gain. They were in the import and export trade business of fine furniture. Before fleeing to France, however, Herr Metlevev had fought for the Russians on the Eastern Front against the Germans in the Great War. It was during this time that Metlevev had an incredible, life-changing experience. He was saved, after a brief but vicious fight with a small German battalion, from certain imprisonment or even death by a horribly deformed enemy soldier named Ludwig Schmidt. Metlevev had at first tried to kill Schmidt, but failed. Instead, Schmidt rescued him. This act of benevolence, a German soldier helping a Russian, was a dangerous act, and Ludwig Schmidt could have faced severe consequences had he been found out by officials of his army.

After relaying this information, Monsieur Suave paused for a moment and asked if I knew Ludwig Schmidt. It took several moments for me to remember who he was. Then suddenly, yes, I remembered. Ludwig Schmidt. The messenger boy. The one who rode a bicycle and made it move like a runaway horse. According to Herr Maier, Ludwig Schmidt had suffered terrible burns as a child, which left his face severely disfigured. Yes, Ludwig Schmidt came to Maier's Chocolate Shop—where I worked as a sales person, before Otto swept me away with his charm—every Thursday to relay messages and provide parcels for Herr Maier. I remember Ludwig Schmidt's eyes; he used to wear dark glasses, but when he came into the chocolate shop he would always take them off. Yet I never saw his face. He always kept it covered with a shawl. His eyes, though, were remarkable! They were blue and bright. When they looked at me I saw warmth, courage, humor, and goodness. I always smiled at Ludwig's eyes. They were beautiful and I felt beautiful when they looked at me. This exchange, this eye contact was extremely brief each time, no more than two or three seconds, but I will always remember it. I tried talking to Ludwig Schmidt a few times, but he never seemed to be able to respond. Physically we looked into each other's eyes, but emotionally we glimpsed into each other's hearts every Thursday, over several months, until one day another messenger appeared. Later, from Herr Maier I ascertained that Ludwig Schmidt had been conscripted by the German army and was fighting on the Russian Front.

There was a long moment of silence in the drawing room once it had been confirmed that I knew Ludwig. Monsieur Suave broke it by saying that during the Great War, Ludwig Schmidt had brought his wounded master to a hospital disguised as a German soldier. Herr Metlevev was operated on by a German doctor and this had saved his life. The doctor had been led to believe by Ludwig Schmidt that Metlevev was a fellow countryman. After recovering Metlevev had feared that his true identity would eventually be discovered, so he fled the hospital one night with Schmidt's satchel. His hope was that there would be money in it, but instead he had found a cardboard tube with several letters rolled up inside. Metlevev proceeded to pull out several documents from his attaché case. They were all letters, written to me, by Ludwig Schmidt. The address of Maier's Chocolate shop was written on the top of each letter. Metlevev said that he could not read German, but he had realized they must be significant and had kept them. A few years later he had Suave interpret the letters for him.

Frankly, I was a little skeptical about all this and asked, with a trace of indignation, why Metlevev had come to me! Should he not have returned the satchel to Herr Ludwig Schmidt first and let him send the letters to me personally, or if that had failed, why not send the letters to Herr Maier and then he could have passed them on to me? By the time I had finished asking these questions I was extremely perturbed. These men had not followed proper decorum!

Metlevev gently waved my indignation down with his right hand and, through Suave, said that Ludwig Schmidt was dead.

"Dead! How could you know?" I demanded harshly.

Metlevev, now quite aware of my wavering mental state, for his face registered concern, slowly rose to leave. Monsieur Suave did likewise. As Herr Metlevev carefully put on his gloves, he looked down at me and through his valet declared, "Herr Maier advised me it might not be wise to see you so soon after your husband's death, and for that I am truly sorry. Out of respect for you I will now bid you adieu. But I do know Ludwig Schmidt is dead because I watched him die. I held his hand till it became cold. I came here to honor the memory of the man who saved my life and to appease my guilt for stealing what are obviously treasured letters. Ludwig Schmidt also referred to you as 'Angel.' Frankly, I was very curious to see why he called you that. Now that I have met you it is very clear why my savior called you an angel. You are, even in your distress, lovely. To have simply sent the letters to you or Herr Maier would not have been respectful to Herr Schmidt, or his angel. I only knew Ludwig Schmidt briefly, but I agree he had remarkable eyes. They conveyed God's love. He was a good man. Good day, Frau Hitzlenberger."

The Russian bowed while the Frenchman once again brushed his lips over each side of my face. The men turned to go, but I had one more question. "Why didn't Ludwig Schmidt send the letters to me during the war?" The men stopped briefly before Suave responded, "The answer is in the letters. We will let you read that for yourself." With that the two foreigners left.

I collapsed on a couch with Ludwig Schmidt's letters in my hands. The visit from these two odd men had drained much emotional energy out of me. I stared at the letters for a long time. Finally I picked one up and started reading. Within minutes I was lost in the words of Ludwig Schmidt.

For several months I read and reread his letters at least a hundred times. Ludwig Schmidt's words revitalized my spirit and brought light into my life. I could pray again. Yet, through the whole time I spent reading Ludwig Schmidt's letters I never considered sharing the contents of his letters with anyone. Partly because they were addressed to me, but mainly because Ludwig's love for me comes through time and time again. Indeed, a grieving widow sharing the love letters of someone she only knew from a distance seemed wholly inappropriate.

Yet a year and a half later, in a rather vain and silly attempt to gauge the commitment of a man seeking my hand in marriage, I allowed

Herr Günter Steinbach to read through the letters. Instead of a jealous response, one that I was anticipating, he quickly advised me to make the letters available to anyone who might need words of encouragement. Certainly it was what God would want and he believed what Ludwig Schmidt would consent to. My mouth dropped in surprise, but Herr Steinbach made great inroads to my heart that day.

Needless to say, I am now engaged to be married to Herr Günter Steinbach and with his blessing I have sent a selection of Herr Schmidt's most stirring and unique letters to you. Herr Schneider, I entrust you to bring the words of Ludwig Schmidt to the lonely, broken hearts of our world, for I am convinced that they will bring light, life, and healing to them as they did mine.

God Bless You,

Elise von Hitzleberger

30 June 1922

From the files of Albrecht Schneider

Dear Reader,

Initially, I received Elise Hitzlenberger's request and "love letters" with little interest. There is really no logical explanation for this; suffice to say that art is a very subjective business and Elise Hitzlenberger's "art" simply did not captivate me. After a short, uninspired look at a few of Ludwig Schmidt's letters I, out of respect for my former business associate's widow, had my secretary send a nice letter to Elise Hitzlenberger vaguely promising a consideration of the proposal she had sent me at some time in the future. This was a polite way of declaring, "I am rather busy and will have forgotten you and what you wrote after I have ordered my secretary to write you a considerate thank you letter for your efforts."

Yet, a week later I had, much to my amazement and amusement, become very curious about something in Ludwig Schmidt's letters. Another week passed and my curiosity had grown to a point where I had to take action.

Through some personal connections in the German government I was able to ascertain the whereabouts of *Pastor* Heribert Lichtwasser without too much difficulty. By the following Saturday, I was traveling on a train from my home in Hamburg to the quaint city of Celle. Upon my arrival I found a little Gasthaus and turned in early. The late May weather was beautiful, and the gentle, flower-scented breezes helped me sleep soundly.

Sunday morning in Celle was heralded by a cacophony of church bells ringing simultaneously. The ringing roused me out of my blissful stupor and, although regular attendance at church was not a major life requirement of mine, I grudgingly changed into my best suit and headed to the nearby Lutheran Church. I chose this church not because I had heard an excellent endorsement for it, but for the fact that it was led by a certain pastor named Heribert Lichtwasser.

The pews were filled to capacity when I entered the sanctuary. Obviously Pastor Lichtwasser had garnered a great following, so I was "banished" upstairs to the back of the balcony by an old, rotund, over-polite but firm usher, who through his facial expressions, tone of voice, and body movements made it abundantly clear that he took his ushering very seriously.

The singing and heartfelt worship of the congregation eased the feelings of apprehension that I had gained from the usher and the bold decision to attend a service with complete strangers. The worship ended and the pastor strode up to the pulpit. He introduced himself as Pastor Lichtwasser (Lightwater), which I thought was a great name for a man of God, considering the significance of light and water in the Christian faith.

Fifteen minutes into Lichtwasser's sermon, fatigue, caused by my travels and the ungodly early hour of the bells ringing me out of my sleep, overwhelmed me. Leaning back on the hard pew with arms crossed, my eyelids hung heavy. Even though Pastor Lichtwasser spoke well, with great confidence and enthusiasm, my drowsy head was only catching a portion of what he was saying: "Ludwig Schmidt...Schmidt...Great War...taught me about Jesus...." Wait. Like a thunderbolt crashing through the roof of the church, my mind lit up. What great fortune. On the one and probably only Sunday that I would attend church for the year, the pastor was talking about a man who I was very intent on knowing more about.

Pastor Lichtwasser's praise for Ludwig Schmidt was extravagant. He was obviously, according to the pastor, one of the greatest men he had ever met. Now completely engaged and intrigued, I absorbed every word that the pastor uttered.

At the end of the service I rushed by my usher friend, whose perturbed gasp at my rate of speed indicated disapproval. However, my eagerness to meet Pastor Lichtwasser overrode polite discretion. I came up to him, introduced myself, and without hesitation asked if I could have an audience with him that afternoon to discuss Ludwig Schmidt. Lichtwasser was very hesitant, mumbling something about protocol, there was an opening to meet a week Tuesday, and so on. Other people in his flock were pressing him for attention and he politely dismissed my efforts. My fat usher friend had managed to arrive near his shepherd and one look at his blustery face was all the information I needed about how welcome I was now at this church. Not much.

In desperation, I raised my voice over the after-church talk and clamor and said, "Ludwig Schmidt killed Sergeant Schwarz!" Never in my life have I ever witnessed such a quick and complete stop in noise and movement amongst a group of people as I did then. Lichtwasser's congregation stared at me, silent and aghast with incredulity. Incredible. Emboldened, I also declared, "Furthermore, I know that you were their commanding officer and you have some responsibility for what happened."

Lichtwasser held out his hand and with a thin smile said, "Who are you?"

"Albrecht Schneider. I am acquainted with Elise Hitzlenberger, otherwise known as Angel. I have the letters written to her by Ludwig Schmidt. Blackbeard, actually a Russian man named Metlevev, gave them to her. He was at the same hospital where Ludwig died."

Now obviously shaken, Lichtwasser stuttered, "Meet me next door at my residence for tea at 2:30."

I gratefully replied, "Thank you."

Lichtwasser started talking to one of his flock and the congregation relaxed and came back to life. Before I could cause another spectacle I was ushered out, on the double, by the plump and very serious usher. Taking a glance back once I was safely out on the sidewalk, I observed with a touch of bemusement that the usher was on the top step of the church, hands on his hips, lips turned into a snarl, eyes radiating fire at the one who had created such a stir in his world. I am sure there is a place in heaven for ushers, hopefully not too close where I will end up.

I arrived, like a good German, punctually at Pastor Lichtwasser's residence at exactly 2:29. The pastor's wife, a blond, lovely woman named Hilda, welcomed me at the front door, and then led me around the house to the backyard. Lichtwasser was dozing on a large, comfortable chair in the shade of a massive apple tree. Upon my arrival he roused himself, shook my hand while giving a sharp nod with his head, and guided me to a nearby patio where a few chairs and a table laden with strawberry torte and tea stood.

Lichtwasser offered me a chair, sat down on one nearby, smiled at his wife, who then wished us a good afternoon and went back into the house. While the pastor was serving me torte and tea he opened the conversation by stating, "Hilda is a wonderful wife. We are expecting our first child in a few months."

"Congratulations," I offered.

"Thank you. Do you have a wife?"

"No, I am afraid marriage has eluded me, Pastor."

"So not even an angel has caught your eye?"

We laughed gently and nodded at the inside joke.

Lichtwasser smiled a moment before saying, "You certainly got the attention of my congregation this morning."

"I apologize for my abruptness, Pastor. That was very unbecoming of me."

"Thank you. I normally do not have visitors Sunday afternoon, so you had to say something rather outlandish or important to get my attention."

"Yes, indeed."

"So why does Ludwig Schmidt interest you?"

"Let us just say his letters to his angel intrigue me. They did not at first, but now I am finding them so interesting that I am considering getting them published. Of course this has been approved by Elise Hitzlenberger."

"Of course. Are you a publisher, Herr Schneider?"

"No, but I do know a few who are inclined to listen to me."

"Is that so?"

"Yes, and I think the story of Ludwig Schmidt would interest them."

"Why?"

"It is a great story. A man, against great odds, makes something out of his life. There are life and death struggles, love, treason, and murder."

Lichtwasser sighed grimly. "So you have proof that Ludwig Schmidt murdered Sergeant Schwarz?"

I pulled out several letters from my attache case and said, "I received these letters that Ludwig Schmidt wrote to Elise Hitzlenberger. You knew her as Angel. Mrs. Hitzlenberger in turn had received them from a man named Metlevev who Ludwig rescued in the war. Apparently Blackbeard, as Ludwig called him, escaped from the German hospital with the letters before anyone realized he was Russian."

Lichtwasser nodded and said with a smile, "It does not surprise me that Ludwig would save an enemy soldier. He was a great man."

I handed Lichtwasser Ludwig's letter to Elise with all the details about how he had killed Schwarz. The pastor read it without expression. Then he slowly laid the letter down on the coffee table and quietly said, "I have not spoken about what happened in that grove to anyone, not even my wife. Yet, I believe with the exposure of Ludwig's letters it is time that I do. I think it will do me and others good."

"You can trust me, Pastor, that what you have to say I will keep confidential."

"Thank you, but I think enough time has passed. Those who were involved with this event, including Schwarz's mother, are long dead. I give you permission to publish anything you want from our conversation, for Ludwig Schmidt was a good cyclist and a great man. His story is inspirational and needs to be told."

"Thank you."

Lichtwasser and I shook hands with a head nod. The pastor picked up the letter from the table, studied it for a moment, then took a deep breath and started a most fascinating narrative.

"According to this letter Ludwig Schmidt did not follow an order from a superior officer and killed him as well. Any one of those two acts was punishable by death during the Great War. As his commanding officer I would have had Schmidt executed if he had confessed to any of these crimes."

"Confession? Did you think he was guilty of treason and murder when he wanted to tell you the truth of what happened in the grove?"

"Before I answer that, let me tell you a little story."

"Please do."

Lichtwasser pursed his lips and reflected quietly for a long time before continuing in a subdued voice. "One day I observed Schmidt taking a bayonet off a rifle. He slid it up his sleeve. The cyclist was in a trench and did not notice that I was watching from above. I followed him discreetly to his next destination. When he stopped in front of Sergeant Schwarz I knew at once what he had in mind. I called out his name, but Schmidt did not respond. I yelled his name again and when he turned to look at me, his blue eyes, which were normally full of warmth, were ice cold. Frightfully cold.

I gave him an order and that was the end of it. But I remember the look on Schwarz's face as he watched Ludwig climb out of the trench. There was a glimmer of fear in his eyes, and that was the only time I ever saw the sergeant look even remotely intimidated.

Later that day Ludwig Schmidt saved our lives. His actions earned him an Iron Cross. It takes great strength to not hurt someone who is treating you cruelly. I knew Schwarz was being inhumane to Schmidt, but I decided that for him to grow into a man he needed to deal with the sergeant in his own way and time. The harsh reality of our situation was that we needed both Schwarz and Schmidt for our survival. I had to be ruthlessly pragmatic during the war. As long as they were doing their jobs to the best of their abilities and helping us survive that was all that really mattered."

Lichtwasser stopped talking and there was a brief respite before I said, "Yet your respect and courtesy to Ludwig Schmidt changed his life for the better. So it is hard for me to believe that you did not care about his problems."

Another long pause ensued before Lichtwasser sighed, nodded, and finally admitted, "With hindsight comes truth. You are right. Schmidt was a genuinely good man, and I respected not only his abilities to do his duties but his character as well. Shortly after the trench incident, I convinced Speck to place Schwarz on a permanent patrol unit, thus keeping the two men away from each other. It also benefited the company, but it actually benefited my friend the most."

"Your friend?"

"Yes, Ludwig Schmidt was my friend."

Lichtwasser slowly took a sip of tea, and with a voice laced in sadness declared, "The truth is I did not want my friend to confess the truth because I would have then been obligated as his commanding officer to have him arrested and executed. To not do so would have been treason and punishable by death on my part. I have known that Ludwig Schmidt killed Sergeant Schwarz since the day we picked him up from the grove. We found Ludwig unconscious with his rifle across his body. I checked the rifle. Only one bullet had been shot from it. Schwarz was dead nearby, with one bullet hole in his forehead. There had been lots of crossfire in the grove during the battle. It is impossible that one perfect head shot from the crossfire would have killed Schwarz. No, there would have been multiple gunshot wounds if he had stood up in the crossfire. Yet, I knew Ludwig would never have killed Schwarz unless under duress. The letter you have allowed me to read confirms this. The truth is Schmidt saved his life by shooting Sergeant Schwarz. When you consider the circumstances Ludwig Schmidt was in, it was the only option for his survival. In my opinion he overcame the evil against him with good. I believe God gave him the opportunity to survive and he took it. Otherwise Ludwig would have died needlessly at the hands of someone who in the heat of battle was panicking and became unreasonable. The other good that came out of this was that I could report the honorable death of Schwarz to his mother and my superiors. Schwarz's mother was the only one in the world who cared about him. She tried to love him as best as possible. I believe that to have told her the truth would have unnecessarily compounded the grief that she was already feeling toward a son who was in many ways emotionally unsound. To say that Sergeant Schwarz died honorably was an expression of compassion to a woman who had suffered too much in her life. The truth was that Sergeant Schwarz, despite his horrible flaws— which, outside of his mother, prevented him from having any meaningful relationships—had from a military perspective served his company and country with distinction. Schwarz's mother needed to know that her son did not die in vain like her husband."

"Very noble. Your friendship with Ludwing Schmidt was deep. To know that he had killed Schwarz yet not charging him for it, thereby risking your own career and life, shows an incredible trust and respect for him."

"He earned it. I believe in this case that the evil of Schwarz was overcome by good. Yet I am not God, and He will judge if what Schmidt and I did was right."

"Anyone else know about the single bullet hole in Schwarz's head?"

"No, I do not think so. There were many bodies and survivors to collect. I don't think anyone noticed what I had."

"Is there a possibility of the military or anyone charging you now for what you did?"

Lichtwasser smiled wryly. "Like I mentioned earlier, Herr Schneider, it has been a long time since World War I. Everyone concerned in this case, including Schwarz's mother, is dead. The battlefield, Herr Schneider, is a horrible place. Rules of the civilized world do not apply. The German military is at present, due to the Versailles Treaty, virtually non-existent. No, I am sure I have nothing to fear about legal retribution. It has been healthy for me to talk. Thank you."

"Tell me what happened after Ludwig died."

"When I received notification that Ludwig Schmidt had died, I ordered three soldiers to take Aunt Bertha and retrieve the corpse and any personal belongings of the late cyclist. Ludwig's body was delivered promptly to me, but his satchel, which had been near his hospital bed, had mysteriously disappeared. One of the nurses believed it may have been taken by the man with the black beard, who had simply vanished shortly before it was determined that Ludwig Schmidt had died.

I attempted to find and inform relatives of Schmidt's passing, but even though a few were found through the war office, no one wanted to take responsibility for his burial. So on a cold February afternoon I had Ludwig Schmidt, Private, Bicycle Brigade, recipient of the Iron Cross (First Class) buried with full military honors and decorum next to the grave sites of Speck and Schwarz. All that remained of the 31st Company attended. Many cried. There were several touching eulogies. Ludwig Schmidt was greatly admired as a man of extraordinary strength. He was a good listener, a good friend, a good soldier, and a good cyclist. No one mentioned his deformity. We all had reached a point where we saw the man, not the skin. And what we saw was good."

The rest of the conversation that sweet May afternoon revolved around Lichtwasser. After surviving several intense battles against the Russians, Kommandant Lichtwasser was eventually captured by them and sent to a prisoner of war camp in Siberia. He survived a harrowing year under inhumane conditions by capturing and eating rats. While en route to another camp he managed to escape into the thick Siberian forest. The story of how Pastor Lichtwasser survived is worthy of a book. Suffice to say he managed to return back to Germany at war's end.

Inspired by his miraculous survival and the life of Ludwig Schmidt, Heribert Lichtwasser became a Lutheran minister. Over the last few years he had learned that out of the 150 original soldiers of the 31st Company, 23 had survived the Great War and were all, in various stages, rebuilding their lives.

The shadows of late afternoon heralded my imminent departure. Pastor Lichtwasser and Hilda refused to let me return to my Gasthaus without spending an evening meal with them. It was almost dark when I finally bid my hosts farewell and headed back to my quarters.

The decision to pursue publication of Ludwig Schmidt's letters to Elise was made that evening. The lesson that human beings are capable of great evil but are also capable of great good is one that cannot be told enough. With God's help man can spend his lifetime doing good, bringing hope, joy, dignity, and blessing to those around them. That is the legacy of Ludwig Schmidt. Ludwig Schmidt was a good man.

About the Author

Dirk Budwill has been a Christian for over thirty-five years.   He is married to Celia and they have a two year old son named Aaron. Dirk and Celia are international school teachers in Hong Kong, China. Previous books written and published by Dirk include *Win Win Tag Games*, *Wolfland*, and *The Probation of Gregory Wolf Sharp*. Dirk was born in Germany but raised in Canada.   He has also lived in the United States and Austria.

Dirk can be contacted at dirkbudwill@gmail.com.